TIME VACATION

TIME VACATION

Leif J. Erickson

UNITED STATES OF AMERICA

Copyright(©) 2014
Millennium Publishing Company

ISBN: 978-0-9960818-3-2

TIME VACATION

Chapter 1

All of the staring was making Quest nervous. Every direction he turned, villagers quickly glanced down. Not quickly enough, though, to hide their curiosity in the two strangers that had appeared in their grassy, hillside hamlet. These people were not used to visitors, it seemed.

"We're drawing to much attention to ourselves," Quest muttered under his breath.

"Relax. Our outfits match the kingdom's colors perfectly." Ron attempted to calm his partner.

"They know," Quest responded. "They definitely know."

"Impossible."

His confidence came from an inner reservoir of past successes, but there were external reasons for the bravado as well. A few of Ron Hess' characteristics merited particular attention. His bald head, acting as something of a Medieval billboard, gleamed in the sun that had just peaked out of the heavy British clouds. His height was another thing. People were a bit shorter, on average, in those times. Ron, on the other hand, would not have looked unusual in the modern day of steroid-fueled athletes; amongst a crowd of barely-fed peasants, his girth marked him as a pale imitation of a giant. And, these villagers were from the past, not some mythical land of make-believe. To them, Ron was a sight to behold.

Ron's physical appearance was really nothing compared to the shiny things on Quest's nose. It was difficult for even these knowledgeable time travelers to remember and anticipate all of the details. Even the most experienced of historical advisors took things for granted, small things of modern times that could mark a visitor and ruin a trip. Though many of the older men and women hunched into walking sticks could certainly have used them, most of these villagers had never seen a pair of glasses. And, they wondered what was happening with the skinnier fellow that seemed to have an extra set of eyes.

Ron was right. The colors were right on the money. But, these visitors might as well have been from Mars, so strange and unusual did they appear to those villagers. For goodness sake, Ron and Quest were the only people in eyesight that had anything close to all their teeth!

"Come on," Ron said to his nervous compatriot.

As they walked, they saw the kinds of things middle schoolers read dry descriptions of in musty textbooks. The thatched roofs made of yellowed grasses. The streets were more pathways of mud than cobblestone. The donkeys were muddied up to their knees, flecked with flies and active with their tails in the search for relief from those pests. The children snaggletoothed and in tattered clothes, were curious and fearless.

"Kids are the same whenever and wherever," Quest said with his first smile of this trip.

"Yep," Ron answered. "Nosy, noisy, and dirty."

"Humph." Quest grimaced just a bit; he'd meant something more positive. He'd been thinking of nieces and nephews with whom he loved to get down on the ground and play make believe.

They walked down those muddy streets and, around the corner of one of the dwellings, they looked out upon a vast field of grass. Goats and cattle roamed freely, amidst their feet strutted chickens, guineas, and even a turkey. But, Ron and Quest stared past those pastoral sights toward, what was in many ways for their company, a money shot.

"There it is!" Ron said excitedly. His tone adopted a mixture of nostalgia and greed, "Perfect."

In Ron's defense, it *was* easy to interpret the energy as the real thing. But, as they walked closer and closer, it became clear that he'd misinterpreted.

"Well…close to perfect," Quest said.

Ron followed close behind, "Oh, you're right. Close to perfect. They are just practicing."

Ron and Quest walked to around 15 feet away from the action. Pausing before they got too close, they watched the two extravagantly clad knights as their swords flashed and clanged. Their undercoats were drenched around the neck and backs with sweat. The sounds these men were making undermined the glamour of the visual from further back. Up close, this struggle was all grunts and heavy breathing—not heroic so much as workmanlike. But, the swords were most certainly real. The sounds made as steel met steel were unmistakable. To Ron, they sounded almost exactly like money in the bank.

When the knights paused, breathless with their efforts, they looked over to look towards their audience. They were either less surprised by the sight of Ron and Quest than the villagers or better at hiding it. Quest imagined that it was the former. These knights had a wider range of experiences than their poorer and less well-traveled time counterparts. Unlike the impoverished peasants, they had probably seen other countries. In travels, they may even have encountered those exotic folk from the Far East, with their powerful spices and breathtaking silks. They would have seen followers of Muhammad with their extravagant prayer rugs and curved swords. At any rate, they did not look surprised to see a broad shouldered balding man. And, they gave no second glance to the spectacles on the lean and stringy haired fellow standing before them. Quest was remembering vaguely that glasses might just have been invented around this time in Italy. Maybe they'd seen a pair in an earlier journey.

"Hello!" the taller knight greeted the visitors, "and welcome to the land of Lord Geoffrey."

"Greetings!" Ron answered. "You all look like you are getting in some valuable practice."

"Have to stay sharp," the shorter and bearded knight replied. "Never know when the King will get the urge to take on those bloody neighbors again.

"Ha!" Quest laughed at the joke, "We wondered if you all might be preparing for a tournament of some sort."

"Word has not been spread of games good sir. No tourneys forth coming that I know of around these parts," the taller knight answered. "We had one four months prior, but I don't know that any of the nobles has an aim to put on another any time soon. Rather expensive extravagance in tight times like these. Harvest was bad around here last season."

"Oh, sorry to hear that." Ron answered. "Drought?"

"Unfortunately we were blessed with too much rain. Or, rain at the wrong times. The heavens opened right after planting season. Washed everything out."

"Hmm, well, the fields look good now. Looks to be a promising harvest this year."

"Hopefully," said the shorter knight.

"Okay, well, we don't want to disturb you anymore. Good day to you both!"

"Good day," they replied.

As they walked away, Ron said to his counterpart, "Would sure be nice if we could find a tournament."

"We already have a couple of those in the pipeline," Quest answered.

"Yeah, but tournaments are like money. You can hardly have too much of it," Ron said mischievously.

"That may be true..." said Quest reluctantly.

"You got it," Ron laughed. "Hey," he pointed, "See what I see?"

"Yeah, but our window is closing. Let's keep a low profile for the next five minutes, ensure a clean transition."

"Aww, Quest! Where is your sense of adventure? From a business perspective, where is your sense of efficiency? We are here. Might as well check on the most valuable possibilities. Let's go," he ordered as he set off towards a small castle.

"Geez!" Quest huffed as he followed. *What does he even think he'll find there? This is a middling castle in a boring place. Nothing stunning ever happens here.*

"Think they'll just let us come in to take a peak?" Ron asked behind him. "Let's ask them for the grand tour."

"Are you kidding? Of course not. They have those walls and guard turrets for a reason, Mr. Hess! There is no way they are going to let a couple strangers just stride in."

"Well, it's worth asking, right?"

"No, it isn't. Chances are we'll be shackled and staked and we won't be able to get to the doorway when it opens. You know what the rules say. Always leave a bit of room for error."

"Of course I know what they say!" Ron answered. "I had a hand in writing them. We'll be fine. I want to see inside those walls. Could be a gold mine!"

"Ahh," came the sound from the bespectacled man.

"Where is your sense of adventure, Quest?"

"I'm a science advisor, sir. We typically don't have much of that sense."

"Too true, Quest. Too true! But, the fact that it is true doesn't mean you shouldn't try to change it."

"I'll work on it, Mr. Hess."

They approached the walls and found a guard wearing plenty of armor and a stern look.

"Hello, good sir!" The guards standing in front of the great door responded to this greeting with silent glares.

"Hello!" repeated Ron.

Silence still.

"Mind if we come take a look around?" Ron asked casually as he continued walking through the door.

"Halt!" Ron and Quest both froze at the order.

"Who are you?"

"I am Ron of the Hess and this is my travel partner, Quest. We seek an audience with the Lord of this beautiful land."

"Well," the guard answered, "we have never heard of you; likely you are two of Henry's men."

"I assure you," Ron said, "that we do not know anyone named Henry, much less serve him."

"And what assurances can you give us?"

"My word as a Lord," Ron said. "Now step aside and let us pass!"

"No good," the second guard huffed. "To the dungeons!"

"Great," Quest muttered. "I told you that this was a bad idea."

Once they were chained to the walls, and the guards had slammed the door, Quest glared over at Ron, "Told you. If they'd decided to just run us through rather than arrest us, we'd have died in this straw covered hellhole. And, I'm not wild about hanging out down here. We may have rid our society of the plague, but it is alive and well during these times. No better place to catch it than from rat poop in a dungeon."

"Hah!" Ron ignored Quest, "Can't believe they didn't accept *my word as a Lord* as currency or proof! Don't I look lordly!"

"Geez, Mr. Hess."

"Quest, again with the worrying. If my watch still works here…the door will open in just a second."

Almost on his word, a rectangle of light, complete with a doorknob, appeared between the two of them.

"Told ya!" Ron said cheerfully. "This place might be an option! On to stop number two."

#

As they stepped through the door, it was almost like awakening from surgery in a brightly lit operating room; the light was so overpowering. This new room had its own sounds: jungle birds and screaming primates. The smell was different too. Whereas the dungeon had smelled musty and damp, this site smelled of honeysuckle and fresh rain.

"Ahh," both travelers relished the change, and squinted at the change in light.

As he rubbed his eyes, Quest couldn't help but be stunned as he looked out off the bluff upon which he and Ron had suddenly appeared. Their backs were to a cliff face, the walls of which were shrouded in honeysuckle. But, it was a type of honeysuckle a bit new to him. The blooms were less yellow than pinkish. Bees and butterflies hovered all around them.

They stood upon a broad rock platform, a convenient natural viewing place. In front of them, a hundred feet down the sheer rock wall, was a lush valley. In that valley, to their left, was a gentle slope with a trickling stream. It emptied out into a small pond that was at Ron and Quest's 12 o'clock. And, around that pond was a sight that had left every test visitor so far slack jawed and breathless. Even though Quest knew what to expect, he still rubbed his eyes at the sight. A pair of triceratops were slowly backing up. After they'd created a distance of about 50 yards, they started lumbering towards each other almost simultaneously. After just a few stubby but quick strides, they rammed each other with a brutality Quest had never seen on the movie screen, much less in life. Both creatures shook their heads, stunned with the force. The sound was like a grenade exploding underwater, but right next to you. It was muted, but fierce. The force was amazing.

As that sound echoed across the valley, they backed up again. They repeated the same actions as before, proving that the force with which they struck each other first was no fluke. On the fourth time, one of the three horns eluded the defensive plates of the triceratops on Quest's right. Blood immediately spewed out of the wound. Amazingly, he seemed unaffected by the carnage. He just backed up again and readied himself for another charge. His counterpart didn't display any outward excitement about momentum. They both seemed content with the reality that they'd ram each other most of the day, and that eventually one of them would win.

In the distance, even larger dinosaurs grazed. Brontosauri, with their elegant necks and massive bodies, almost like a combination cow and giraffe, but each was larger than a city bus. They seemed oblivious to the struggles of those two aggressive males beside the pond. They did not even deem to look in the direction of that fierce battle, focusing instead on the leaves of the massive trees around which they were gathered.

"Hah!" Ron said. "Still here. I told you this new site was perfect!"

"It is stunning," Quest agreed. "Last time I visited, when the exploratory committees were still perfecting the locale, we were down closer to the lake. But, we could hardly see those triceratops from the trees. And, we barely escaped before a little raptor-like creature charged us. We were lucky, in fact, that he didn't make it through the door as we squeezed through!"

"A fierce dinosaur, confused and alone, might not have worked out so well in the office," laughed Ron.

Quest nodded his agreement. "No, but this is perfect. The view from up here on this cliff is really stunning."

"This," Ron said, "is why they pay us the big bucks!"

"It is easy to see why people would want to see this," Quest responded. "My seventh grade self would have fainted with excitement to see real, live dinosaurs."

"That is a good point!" Ron said.

"What's that?" Quest responded quizzically.

"Your seventh grade self...we don't often think of children as customers. But, I want to make sure we arrange our business structures so we can be as efficient as possible. No customer should be too small. No money too little for our energy and attention. Everyone is a customer of Time Vacation. We have options that appeal to all ages!"

"Well," Quest said slowly, "I like the idea of making this stuff more affordable. But, with kids, you'd have to make sure to keep things safe. And, they can be so much more unpredictable. I can't imagine bringing school trips or anything."

"School trips!" Ron answered. "Now, you are talking. That is a great idea."

"I don't know, Mr. Hess. And," Quest continued, "with more numbers, I just think you run so much more risk of accidents. I don't know how you can prepare thousands of people for this kind of stuff effectively. The preparation process is so important, and I don't know that you can scale that kind of thing safely."

"Again with the negativity, Quest! You might use some business terms every now and then, but you have no spirit! I want more sites! I want to diversify our offerings so that we can appeal to people other than millionaires. We may be selling the past, but our future has no limit if we do this right."

"Hmm," Quest sighed to himself, not willing to argue any more than he already had. He didn't like how flippant and aggressive Ron could be, but he did like his job. He knew that he should keep his mouth shut if he wanted to keep it.

"Alright," Ron said as he looked at his watch, "Next stop is the last for the day. Ready?"

"Ready," Quest answered. A door flashed before them once again. They turned the knob, and stepped out of one scene and into another.

#

The new setting was one for which they were poorly dressed. Luckily, they appeared in a dark bar that had no patrons other than the man and woman they were supposed to be meeting.

"Quest," Ron said, "You know Eco and Zone?"

"Of course," Quest replied. "Good to see you both."

"And you," they answered.

"First of all, thanks for finding a quiet place for us to chat," Ron said. "Quest and I have been exploring, and we didn't really have time for a costume change."

"We should be good here. This place doesn't ever have customers. And, when they do, they are soon enough too drunk to cause any problems," Eco said.

"Well, what have you got for me?"

"Glad to see you, Ron," Eco started nervously. She was always a bit timid when giving pitches to the boss. "I think this setting has some opportunities, but..."

"But what?" Ron interrupted her. "Don't give me any of the old excuses."

"Well, this is a sort of stereotypical western town. Old west, you know," Zone spoke up.

"Eco, Zone," Ron paused for effect, "the customers of Time Vacation do not pay for stereotypical. They pay for once in a lifetime. Better yet, they pay for once in the history of the world! They do not pay us for generic crap they can see on a movie screen."

Eco and Zone sat quietly. Neither seemed willing to argue with their boss. Finally, Eco spoke up.

"We know. The problem is, we just haven't found much here...yet."

"Well, guys and gals, do your damn jobs. Have you asked around? Maybe inquired about famous shootouts?"

"Of course," they both answered defensively.

"But," Eco continued, "calendars aren't real big here. And people really are bad with dates, much less times. We have been given some recommendations, which are hard to come by, by the way, when people are suspicious of you from the get-go. But, tracking down the substance of those recommendations has proven less than fruitful. People just don't know when things happened. And, usually they've just heard about stuff second-hand. It isn't like they have the news or anything. Most of them just spew rumors. They haven't seen the stuff they claim to have seen."

"Tall tales, huh?" Ron said. "Well, the good news about that problem is it's one I've heard before. You are pros. You've found me gold before. Do it again. It is, after all, why I pay you. If you want that to keep happening, I'd suggest you find a solution that works. So many of our customers ask about visiting this time period. Every man wants to be either Wyatt Earp or John Wayne, and no one grows up without a game or ten of cowboys and Indians. We really need some extraordinary options from the Wild West."

"We know, Ron," Eco conceded.

"Failure, isn't an option."

"We understand."

"I'm glad you do. Remember it every minute of your increasingly tenuous jobs."

"We'll find something. Promise."

Chapter 2

The day was bright and new, the sun peaking over the high trees surrounding the little cove in which the lead ship sat. Out in the ocean, trolling with nets and moving in a methodical pattern back and forth, were numerous small ships. On each, a captain peered closely at the depth finder in front of him, searching not for fish, but for anything that looked out of the ordinary. The sands of the beaches on this particular island glistened as the sun rose; the grains together were not perfectly white so much as glasslike. They shone like crystals in a chandelier. If only they'd been noticed. The sailors on the ships were not here to take in the sights. They had no time to sun on the perfect shore. They were here for business. They were here for adventure. Neither of those causes left much room for gazing at the scenery.

On the lead ship, out of the surf and in the protective calm of the cove, a swarm of researchers plotted points on maps, readied the exploratory one-man submarine to be sent out again, and generally hurried back and forth with the caffeinated energy of that morning's scalded coffee. In the captain's tower, which was elevated about 10 feet from the main deck, sat three men. They each pored over the map in front of them, quizzically and quietly searching for something that would not reveal itself despite their energy and efforts. They did not speak for minutes. Finally, Dale

Brooks mussed his full head of rusty hair and shrugged his broad shoulders,

"I don't know, guys. But, dammit! It has to be around here somewhere. Dennis, what do you think?"

"Well, we've searched every cove and every natural harbor. Is it possible we missed it? I hate to say it, as what I'm suggesting entails weeks of backtracking, but, should we retrace those steps?" Dennis answered.

Dennis's words were not offered lightly. He was younger than the other two, but his gray hair and bushy beard gave him an air of authority he otherwise might have lacked at this table. His quiet demeanor meant that every word he did offer carried additional gravity. And, he'd just uttered what they'd all been reluctantly thinking. It was not a pleasant or welcomed suggestion.

Brad Hammer had a habit of smoothing his mustache as he talked, perhaps checking to see that his facial hair hadn't abandoned him like his now shaved head. The tic gave the impression of deep thought.

"With the amount of ships those documents talk about, I doubt it could have been missed. And, I'm not just saying that because I want to avoid retracing our steps. I just don't think we could possibly have missed a wreck that size," Brad said.

"I think you are right," Dale agreed. "I'm starting to wonder if it hasn't already been found, years earlier and quietly. Maybe some pirates of sorts made off with it, and wrecked themselves.

With the amount of money to be made here, I'm surprised that no one else has ever looked for it."

"It was secret, Dale. No one was supposed to know about it, save the royal family," Dennis reminded the table.

"I know. I know the story by heart. But, secrets in royal families are usually a bit less effectively guarded than their bloodlines. I find it hard to believe that this information didn't get used for some sort of political machination or personal vendetta. Not even a royal family can lose that sort of treasure quietly. They would have been livid. It would have been a well-publicized disaster. Taxes may have been raised to accommodate for the loss. Presuming that we are actually the first to search, the story tells us that the ships took shelter in a natural harbor, but that the storm was too great and all of them sank."

"Right," Dennis continued, "and some of the men were able to swim to shore before the ocean took them, and they reported back once they made their way back to the Kingdom. If only they'd reported a bit more clearly where they'd sank."

"Hard to blame them," Dale said, "a lot of these Caribbean islands look the same to me. What do you think, Brad?"

"Lots of area to cover is what I think. Lots of uncharted waters out here. These islands are pristine for the same reason they haven't been fully explored—it just takes too much energy to get out here. And, it all depends upon what those original witnesses meant by 'natural harbor.' That phrase could mean any number of things from a sailing perspective."

"It is a massive island chain," Dale agreed. "I for one just hope we are in the right set of landmasses."

"I don't know what choice we have except to keep exploring," Dennis muttered with the air of someone about to undergo a root canal.

"Agreed," Dale and Brad said simultaneously. At that, a phone rang.

"It's mine," Dale said as he reached into his pocket and stepped away from the table.

Brad leaned in to Dennis, "Still think this is doable?"

"I know it is," he replied. "When I found all that stuff in Dad's attic—the journal, logs, and shipping registry from one of the ships, it took me a while to track down the loose ends. But, I'd always heard about a distant ancestor who was a 'brave admiral' and who'd survived a terrible storm when others died. These were the logs from that storm." He gestured to the table in front of them both. "And, they left little doubt as to the priceless value of what went under!"

"List it for me again," Brad said, "just to keep me motivated."

"Two billion dollars worth—in today's money—of gold, silver, and jewels. And that is just the market value of those things. No telling what they'd fetch in a NYC auction house." Dennis paused and smiled greedily, "That is just the things listed. There were priceless artifacts taken, or stolen, from the natives as well."

"Sounds so good when it hits my ears…a treasure to lure anyone indeed."

"Indeed."

"That man," Brad continued as he pointed at Dale, "is a good one to have on your team. Dale does not accept failure and he always figures out a way to succeed."

"I hope you're right," Dennis answered. "I think my father knew how valuable all this stuff would be. After all, he kept all those tattered old documents. He must have had an idea that they were worth keeping for more than sentimental reasons. I'm sure of it. The man didn't have a sentimental bone in his body. He just didn't know what to do with all of this information. I wish he could be here to be a part of this. He loved a good adventure more than he loved bourbon. And…he loved him some bourbon."

"Well, we know what to do with that information. Or, more particularly, he does," Brad said as he looked to Dale again.

Dale's back was to the both of them, but as they stopped talking about the treasure, they could hear the tone of his voice shift. He had grown more and more excited. As he ended the call, Dale turned back to them confidently with a million—or two billion—dollar smile. He strutted back to the table, sat down with them, and looked them both in the eye slowly,

"Gentleman," he said.

"Good news," Dennis asked?

"The best. I knew this would work."

"What do you mean? We've been searching for weeks, no sign of the wrecks," Brad responded. "What could you have learned over the phone that could help?"

"Well, now, I have a plan. I needed one more person to fulfill it. And, that phone call was from all the way back in New York City. Turns out, I've got my man. More specifically, I've got my woman!"

"What do you mean?" Dennis asked..

"Well, I need to wait and shore things up with her. But, we've been floundering out here in the islands, looking for a very valuable bunch of needles in a big haystack."

"And?" Brad urged him on.

"And, I think I may have just located the foremost expert in the search at hand. She should narrow the scope of this search exponentially! Our haystack might just have gotten a lot smaller."

Chapter 3

The "Time Vacation" sign on the building was, if not ostentatious, at least a bit out of place. Surrounded by the typical, unimposing skyscrapers, the kinds filled with law offices and insurance firms that preferred their real estate non-descript and classy, the "Time Vacation" building would have fit in perfectly. Those other structures were all glass and shiny metal, the stuff that made the window-washing business lucrative. The "Time Vacation" building was not constructed for that company, so it fit in with its neighbors. But the building now wore a particularly galling sign. Amidst that "normal" looking skyline, what people from blocks around noticed was a three story glowing picture of two Tyrannosaurus Rex snarling at each other, which alternated with an image of a soldier dressed in revolutionary era garb aiming a rifle at an enemy. The characters even moved, running in a ten-second loop. The effect was similar to a sign from Times Square being plopped down in the middle of downtown Wichita, Kansas.

It may have been gaudy, but it worked. Into that building, day after day, streamed customers rich and poor, old and young, asking about the words advertised beneath those fighting ancient lizards, "SEE ANCIENT SIGHTS. DINOSAUR FIGHTS. YOUR NATION SIGNING FOR ITS RIGHTS! TAKE A TIME VACATION!"

"I can assure you that this will be the vacation your family treasures for a lifetime," Ron was saying to a family of four inside that structure.

They were in the briefing room, which had smart screen images of famous revolutionary paintings. On the opposite board was a schedule of the day's routine. Out the window flashed a tyrannosaurus.

The two kids, both teenagers, looked thrilled at the description. It sounded so wild, so extravagant. Their father wore the same hopeful expression on his face. The mother alone looked...reluctant. Ron, as he typically did, was preaching to the choir, not to the doubters. In this case, he hardly acknowledged the worried lines on the face of the mother.

"For the history buff, there just is nothing like it. To watch bad actors reenact the scenes on TV just does not do it justice," Ron exclaimed.

The father, Joe, smiled, "I still cannot believe that we are going to see the signing of the Declaration of Independence!"

"Dad," the younger boy said, "You sure you don't want to do the Dinosaurs trip?"

"It is tempting isn't it, Tim? But, I'm sure! I'd rather see famous human beings than prehistoric lizards."

"Big lizards fighting it out sounds cooler in my book. But either way," the son replied, "this is going to be AWESOME!"

"It better be, for how much it costs," the mother muttered quietly. She kept crossing and uncrossing her legs anxiously. She bit her bottom lip so much that Ron worried it might start bleeding.

"One of the great moments in the history of this great nation," Ron ignored her stress and kept selling, "The defining document that allowed us, as a nation, to become what we are today. The document that, in a way, allowed us to create this great company. I doubt that a stubby old monarch would have approved of the risks we had to take to launch this company. In America, we had the freedom to reach for our dreams. Dan Blank had the freedom to take risks, and he was able to get capital investments to pursue those risks. If those things weren't true, he may never have discovered time travel. And, Time Vacation would not exist. And, now, the Johnson family—you!—can go back to see this major event first hand. In a way, you get to see the event that enabled your vacation in the first place!"

The mother, Molly, still biting her lower lip in anxiety, spoke up, "There sure are a lot of rules that we have to remember. What if something goes wrong?"

Now that she could no longer reasonably be ignored, Ron adopted now the voice of a calming doctor, a tone that was aided by his professional looking three piece business suit.

"Never fear. Nothing will go wrong. This company is accredited and highly acclaimed. We've thought of everything so you don't have to. Sure, there are some rules. But, we do that for everyone's safety. We need to make sure we watch history, not alter it. Who could know the long-lasting implications of the smallest change? To ensure that all goes well, we send you with an expert in every field you could possibly need. You'll have a time advisor, a science advisor, and an expert on the time period along for the journey. They can address any problems you face or questions you have. They face the same set of limited risks that you all face, but they do it daily."

Emily, the young teenage girl, spoke up, "Can we interact with anyone there?"

"Unfortunately, no. We just don't want to take any risks. And, as the Declaration is one of our most popular spots, imagine what would happen if everyone started chatting it up with pre-colonial Philadelphians. It could be a mess."

"But," Tim asked, "We do get to walk around the city? And we get to watch the Continental Congress?"

"Sure do," Ron answered proudly.

"And," Molly asked again, "That is all totally safe? This was a dangerous time. What if we pick up some disease that has been eradicated in our world?"

Ron was losing patience with this woman. How fearful can one person be, anyways? This kind of mindset always drove him crazy. Some people would rather sit comfortably at home than go out and see something truly amazing. Those sorts preferred to live in tiny boxes of their own devising rather than having a bit of trust and taking a bit of risk.

In the face of this anger and frustration, he was a businessman first, so he responded as diplomatically as ever.

"Perfectly safe, ma'am. We've never lost anyone on a time vacation before. We have no intention of doing so now. It'd be bad for business!" He winked at the father before continuing, "Trust in the advisors accompanying you, they'll get you back safe and sound. But, before you return, you are going to see something truly and absolutely spectacular!"

The father nodded throughout this soliloquy and nearly shouted right as Ron finished, "Let's go!"

"That's the spirit!" Ron answered.

He then led this family out of the briefing room, down a long hall, and into what looked to be a new-age dining area. As they followed, the women navigated their hoop skirts. The tails on their jackets flapped behind Tim and his father. Time appropriate clothing for a time vacation! Didn't want to stand out. Getting noticed was not the goal of these trips. Actually getting the chance to live and breathe history, as seamlessly as possible, was.

"We have a special dinner prepared for you," Ron said. "The needs of your body must be monitored closely. And, we like to have you all eat meals that we have pre-approved for the process. Once you've eaten, I'll introduce you to Baljeet. Then we'll be putting you in the time pods, and you'll be on your way."

"Awesome," Tim said.

"Indeed!" said Joe.

Every family member scarfed down their food save for the mother, whose doubt seemed to plague even her stomach. Ron watched her eagerly, a bit frustrated at having to wait as she picked at her food bit by tiny bit.

"Come on, Mom! Hurry up."

Once she'd finished the requisite amount of pre-trip calories, Ron invited them to follow him once again, "Just down this hall, stay close with me now. No peeking into other rooms please, Timmy! And just here."

As he opened the door, the Johnson family stared at the new age sleek white pods before them. There were four, and they were identical, save the red markings above the opening that served as the entrance.

"Okay," Ron said. "Everyone, this is Baljeet."

"Good afternoon, Mr. and Mrs. Johnson," Baljeet said, "Tim, Emily, are you two kids ready for history the way you'll never see it in school?"

"Sure am!" Emily said. "And I even liked history in school. So, this is like a dream for me."

"Baljeet," Molly remarked and then looked away from the white-coated assistant to the man she perceived to be his boss, "Ron, I see that these machines are marked either XX or XY."

"Very perceptive," Ron said, trying to encourage her however he could, "That level of attention to detail will serve you well during the vacation. You may remember from high school biology the way that human chromosomes work."

"I wondered if that was what those meant!" Mrs. Johnson replied.

"Sure is," Baljeet chimed up. "It took Dan Blank some time, but he had a major breakthrough when he remembered that old chromosomal difference between male and female. Time travel is a sophisticated physiological process. It works slightly different depending on the internal make-up of the body. Blank found that male and female travelers benefited from slightly different pod—climates. So, each of these pods is uniquely configured for one particular gender. You can see that we have two for the two gentleman, two for the ladies."

"Wow," Tim responded as he walked over to run his hand down the smooth texture of a pod. "No rivets!" He exclaimed.

"Good again," Baljeet said, "You a fan of planes, Tim?"

"Am I ever!" Tim gushed, "I build model planes with my dad all the time, especially during the summers."

"Well, this is a step beyond the average jet," Ron replied. "And maybe even a step above those models! Rivets, joints, all of those would adversely affect travel. These pods are sleeker than any travel mechanism previously engineered."

With all the science and engineering talk, Ron noticed Mrs. Johnson becoming increasingly fidgety. She seemed to reject things more and more vehemently the less she understood them.

"Umm," She started, but Ron cut her off before she could say anything.

"Well, time to load up! Baljeet?"

"Everything is ready, sir," he said as he directed Mrs. Johnson and Emily to those pods marked XX. "This way please," and Tim and Mr. Johnson to those marked XY.

"Okay, Johnson family," Baljeet said after they were all loaded. "What will happen next is straightforward: your doors will close, the journey will feel like it takes about five seconds, and when these doors open again, your time advisors will greet you from the year 1776."

Each of them nodded their agreement and understanding.

Baljeet punched a few buttons, then looked at each of the family members to ask finally, "You ready?"

"Yeah!" Mr. Johnson nearly shouted. "Let's go!"

"Relax and enjoy your trip!" Ron bid them farewell.

At that, Baljeet pushed some additional buttons at his control center. In front of him, he could see video footage of each of the four passengers on separate monitors. Both of the children looked both scared and thrilled, like the average first-rider on a roller coaster as it climbs the first big incline and slows, just before the rush of air and speed. Mr. Johnson wore an expression of calm, deep satisfaction, and almost relief, as if his life of tedium had finally led to something of interest and he was relieved to find it worth living. Mrs. Johnson just looked scared shitless as she bit her fingernails. *I can imagine,* Ron thought, *why he would be excited to do something different and exciting, with a wife like that.*

Baljeet continued his work, increased his typing speed, and finally there was a hum of electricity from each pod and an unmistakable but subtle popping sound. It was like the air had been sucked from the room.

Within two seconds, Baljeet looked down at his control panels, which were blinking green. Each of the bigger dashboard components then beeped once and flashed blue, at which he said to Ron and the room in general, "They made it."

"Good," Ron replied. "Of course they did with you at the controls, Baljeet!"

"Thank you, sir."

"I'm sure they will enjoy their stay."

"Sir," Baljeet said, "You know we in the logistics department can do this stuff. The systems are so well established. Do you worry about us implementing things incorrectly?"

"Of course not! I've nothing but confidence in my people."

"Then, sir, if you don't mind me asking, why do you observe so many of the vacations. I'd think that a CEO might have more important things to do."

"Oh," Ron answered, "I've more than enough to do. And my wife would tell you that I should certainly be spending my time more efficiently. That way, I might get home at a reasonable hour. But, I just can't help myself. I love to watch these passengers before and after. The vacations...I feel like I need to keep reminding myself as vividly as possible what we are doing and why. I started as a salesman. In some ways, I remain one at heart. Nothing helps a salesman more than to see people enjoying the product to be sold."

"And you worry that you might forget about that magic if you don't observe frequently?"

"Budget spreadsheets and council meetings have a way of numbing the brain from all good and positive things," Ron responded.

"Ah," the white-coated assistant nodded sympathetically.

"They didn't look like our typical clients to me."

"The Johnsons?"

"Yes, sir."

"Is that a class observation?" Ron asked sharply.

"Well," Baljeet said, "I guess it was. They seemed a bit less high-brow than most of our clients."

Instead of asking upon what Baljeet had based that presumption, he let it pass. He knew what his assistant was getting at, "Her parents passed away and left them five million dollars. Her father made a single good stock purchase at the right time."

"They spent all of her inheritance on this?" Baljeet asked in a startled tone.

"From the tone of your voice, you do not approve."

"Well, it does seem really extravagant. You know, I didn't grow up wealthy. And, I know how far that money would go for college funds or paying off a mortgage. They could have done so much more. Invested in something that would have helped them long term. That windfall could have changed their lives. They spent it instead on six hours, on a frivolous trip?"

"They make that choice for themselves, Baljeet."

"It's just that," Baljeet started.

"I'm not getting into it with you again." Ron said angrily. "It's their money and their choice." He stormed out.

Baljeet bit his lip, but thought to himself: *It is not their money anymore. And, choice is a relative term with people like that and advertisements designed to do what ours do. It's like cigarette ads and children.* And at that internal analogy he grew angrier, *Jerk!*

Chapter 4

The hotel bar was an exercise in subtle opulence. The lights were dim, but they shone from crystal chandeliers spaced every 20 feet overhead. They shone enough to illuminate the daily-shined brass fittings on the bar, the dark mahogany bar top, the plush chairs surrounding each of the tables draped in newly laundered white tablecloths. It was the kind of place where beautiful people spoke in hushed tones about things they thought were important. But, it was also the kind of place where much of that beauty had been acquired surgically or through the help of private trainers.

Not her, though. She was like something out of a Renoir, save the parasol. She didn't look to belong amongst all the old-money types in this place. She was tall, even sitting down, with a frame that came from youth and athletic exertion. Her dark brown hair framed academic tortoise shell glasses set on a sun-tanned face. She was dressed with an air of class: a fancy skirt stopped just below her knee line, and her blouse revealed just enough cleavage to get the average hot-blooded man's imagination spinning. The beauty on display was enough to overcome even a flushed face and bleary eyes that suggested tears past or tears to come. She was in the mood to sip a fancy martini and numb her frustration. She was not in the mood for suitors. But, when one looks like Becca Baxter, one attracts suitors. She'd known that when she put on the blouse, and it was slightly unrealistic for her to feel frustrated at the attention now.

As surely as a single male sat at the bar to order a single malt or beer, just as surely he'd send a drink her way. When that happened, she'd accept. She acquiesced even though she knew that this offering would soon entail a few minutes of unwanted attention. She dealt with the quick pick-up attempts because they earned her more $15 martinis. Guilt was not a problem; she felt no regret sipping those drinks as she refused their advances coolly, "Thanks for the drink. But, I just want to be alone."

Becca had already sat through this same dynamic a few times when a man walked over to her and offered a drink. By this point she'd had one too many, so she had to think before she responded with the proper mix of diplomacy and firm insistence. As she paused, he spoke up, "You are Becca Baxter, right? I want to be sure I'm buying for the right beautiful woman."

His voice was appealing to her in a way the others had not been. And, he was handsome. But, his words caught her off guard.

"How do you know who I am?" she asked, startled.

"Why don't you just come with me? Maybe we can find a place a bit more…private to chat?"

Mistaking his invitation for an entreaty of another kind, and suspicious regardless, Becca responded dismissively, "I'm just fine here. Who are you?"

"My name is Dale Brooks. And, I have an offer for you."

"I'm not interested."

"Well," he responded with a slight smile. "I wouldn't be either, if I hadn't heard the offer."

"I hear offers all the time," Becca responded. "You are the fourth or fifth tonight."

"Oh," Dale laughed. "Not that kind of offer."

Becca couldn't help but be a bit taken aback. She was also a bit, and this shocked her even as she felt it, offended. *He's not interested?* She thought angrily to herself.

"This has been a rough couple months for you, Ms. Baxter. If I'd undergone such a set of events, I might be drowning my sorrows in gin and vermouth too. You were just fired from the university, right?"

"Yeah…" she said slowly, "But how did you know that?"

"Not only that, you had your last book—what must have been years of work—discredited. That was you too, right?"

The man's leading questions, on this point, just earned him an icy silence. He quickly realized that he might have pushed a bit too hard, "I want to help. I want to offer you a job right now."

"Look," Becca responded, "who the hell are you? How do you know who I am? And how did you know that I would be in this bar?"

"My name is Dale Brooks. We can cover that other stuff later. And, I'm sorry for the gruff start. Let's talk about this job."

"Okay…" Becca responded, a little less cool this time. "But, I'm not some charity case. I just need a month to get back on my feet."

"I'm not offering you charity. I'm offering you hard and interesting work. We've acquired a journal and some shipping logs about some ships that sank in the northwestern side of the Caribbean."

"Well," Becca replied, "that isn't too hard to do. You can buy those things at Sotheby's auctions twice a year. Plus the private market, which is usually humming."

"True," Dale agreed, "but this isn't the kind of journal that would show up at one of those sales. This one has only been seen by a few select people."

"How's that?"

"It sat in someone's attic for the last 50 years. Before that, it was probably in another attic. Bottom line, we believe that a massive treasure awaits the person who can decode all of the admittedly vague descriptions therein. I know...I know...people always think their map will lead them to riches. But, we have actual reasons for believing this will work."

"What would you want from me?"

He waited a beat before continuing, "If you are the Becca Baxter that I've heard so much about, and your appearance certainly matches the glowing reports I'd received from various folks, I can think of no other person who knows more about Caribbean shipping from the settlement times than you."

She dismissed the compliments, "I doubt I could be much help."

"Well, we disagree on that point," Dale said. "But, what do you have to lose? Do you have any other jobs lined up right now?"

"No." She shook her head. "But..." she trailed off.

"Whatever you need for compensation, we can get it."

"That certainly sounds nice," Becca responded. "But, if academics were motivated by money they would have chosen law school instead."

"Right," Dale paused thoughtfully, "What matters to you is writing. How about this? When we are done with this project, which will inevitably make us all very rich and very famous, you can have the exclusive rights to writing about it. You'll live in the main cabin, suntan on the deck all day long, and drink all the martinis you want," he motioned to the long legged stemware in front of her.

"All you have to do in return is make sure we navigate efficiently. We need help finding this site. You are our woman!"

"Well," Becca answered, "I should probably wait to talk more about this tomorrow, when I've had a few more coffees and few less martinis."

"Time is off the essence, Becca. What do you say?"

She smiled mischievously, "When do we start?"

Chapter 5

The sun glared intensely down from its perch, hot enough to roast any human skin foolish enough to spend much time in the rays. Nearby, the pool provided a cool respite from the heat; the umbrellas around the side offered shade. Maximilian smiled quietly to himself as the waiter brought out the next round of fruity drinks. Even the piña colada needed an umbrella in this sun! He thought.

"What's so funny Max?" the blonde asked him.

"Just a thought I had, Lacey." He replied, unwilling to share his private joke with the three women that sat now looking at him. Even if he were so inclined, they wouldn't get it anyway. This heat was normal to them.

He was reclined on a chair, wearing nothing but his swimsuit and shades. The redhead was massaging sunscreen into the top of his muscular shoulders. He had just enough hair on his chest to look truly masculine, but not enough to merit a trip to the salon for waxing. His hairline was a further from his crystal blue eyes than it had been in his teenage years, but he wore it short regardless. His jawline was almost fierce, and his teeth suggested a childhood in which money was readily available for a good dentist. He had an attractiveness to him, but much of his energy came from an air of confident presence. This man was not someone to be trifled with, and he was someone that women enjoyed immensely.

"Waiter, could you bring the ladies here another round?"

"It's only three o'clock, Maximilian," Shawn said, "Are you trying to get us tipsy before dinner?"

"You know it ladies! Then, it's back to the bedroom with you all!"

The waiter stood a bit awkwardly, before asking, "Margaritas again, ladies?"

"Yeah!" they all shouted.

"And another Blue Label for me, please?" Max added.

"You've got it," the waiter replied.

As the waiter made his way back to the bar, Heidi returned to the previous point.

"We love your thoughts, Max!" she said as she paused.

I know you do, he thought a bit hubristically, but said instead, "It was nothing, Heidi. Just something silly."

He wondered if their eagerness to hear what he was thinking might have something to do with jealousy. But, they'd never displayed any traces of that before. They were kind to each other, and had shared some pretty wonderful moments between the four of them, moments about which other girls might have been a bit too bashful, moments that cast doubt on the idea of jealous inclinations. No, it couldn't be that. Probably, it was that vague sense of fear.

"You aren't still planning on leaving tonight Maxi?"

"I am," he responded.

"Don't do that. We are going to miss you so much!"

"I'll miss you all as well."

"We know you will," Lacey said devilishly, "And, we also know that you'll be back. You always come back."

"This time it'll be different," Maximilian said resolutely.

"We've heard that before, too." Heidi said, "And we hope you are wrong this time again."

"I've got fishing to do," Maximilian said. "I'm still searching for that trophy to mount on the wall."

"You can fish in our world, too," Heidi argued. "We'll go to any lake you want, anywhere. And, we'll all be together then."

"That sounds great." Max said, "It really does. And, you all know that I care about you. But, it wouldn't be right. It has to be a lake in my time. I just don't feel right here, as much as I'm torn about leaving you all. But, this will be the last time we see each other. Let's focus less on that and more on our one great day!"

"That's hard, Max," Shawn said with a mopey voice.

"I know. But, can you try for me?" The other two girls looked like they just might cry. He hated to do this to them, but he certainly wanted to be honest.

Finally, Shawn spoke for all three, "Anything for you, darling."

He looked at the other two, and they nodded. They tried to summon up smiles, and together enjoyed a few too many margaritas before heading up to the bedroom together, all holding hands as they walked. That night, after their final hurrah, Maximilian grabbed his bag, kissed them all on the foreheads, and walked out the door.

Chapter 6

On the wall of the Time Vacation building, as the sun went down outside and twilight took hold, the gaudy sign shown all the more brightly: **DINOSAUR FIGHTS**! Inside, behind the newly washed windows, four white pods appeared from another dimension and the doors opened, "How did it go?" Ron asked the Johnson family as they stepped cautiously out of their pods. They seemed disoriented about the fact that they could have so simply and easily reentered the time period in which they'd been born.

Joe spoke first, "It was everything I could have imagined and more."

Even Molly, that most reluctant of mothers, agreed both visually and verbally. She nodded as she gushed, "It was the most wonderful thing of all time. Certainly the most amazing experience of our lives."

"I told you darling," the husband chided.

She glowed as she kissed her husband admiringly, "Thank you honey for taking us on it. It was the trip of a lifetime."

The kids were slightly less dazed. It was always harder to surprise and shock kids in this modern world.

But, Tim agreed, "It was pretty cool. Now I know I'll ace AP history or at least the parts about the Revolution."

"If only it was that simple," his mom laughed.

"They smelled funny," Emily piped up, finally adjusting to her current setting and the question posed initially by Ron.

"Well, you have to remember that they didn't have deodorant. And, whereas you all showered and wore clothes that had been washed in a machine with soap, they didn't have that sort of stuff either. Don't hold it against them!" Ron responded.

"I won't!" Emily said good-naturedly. "After the first few minutes the smell didn't bother me much."

"Where is the trio that was with us?" Joe asked.

"They were so professional and informative. We really liked our guides!" Molly said.

"I'm glad to hear that," Ron said. "I'll tell them you complemented them. They won't be joining us here, though. They stay back for a little longer to make sure we haven't had any long-lasting effect on the time zone during the visit. Once they see that all is all clear, and that we haven't altered history, they'll return in their private pods. Since they do so much traveling, they have custom-made travel units. Trust me, they'll be fine."

At that reassurance, a woman in a white lab coat walked in, her heals clicking on the tile floor as she entered, "Hello Judy," Ron greeted her. "If you all follow Judy here, she'll take you to the bedroom area of the building. Then, once you've had your night of sleep to make sure there are no adverse travel effects, you'll be free to go!"

"What if we want to go back?" Tim asked.

"Tim," his dad said, "don't be greedy. We've got enough to remember for quite a while!"

"Sleep well," Ron said. "We always hear how comfy our beds are. Hope you all have sweet dreams." He laughed as he shook their hands and motioned towards Judy.

"Mr. Hess," Emily stopped he and Judy both.

"Nothing could happen to us, right?"

"Well, like with surgery, there's a small chance that complications can arise with time travel. But, by keeping you here, we will know and be able to correct it before anything happens. Sleep well, rest proudly in knowing that you just did something that very few people will ever be able to claim they did! Sleep the sleep of brave time travelers."

"Thank you, Ron," Joe said. "Thank you so much."

Ron turned to his reluctant and argumentative assistant, "Baljeet, did you see the look on those faces?"

"Yes," he conceded, "They were very happy."

"That is why I do this."

"I wonder if they'll remember that look in 10 years, when they are still struggling under the weight of a second mortgage and college bills."

"I'm betting they will," Ron said confidently.

"Well, I doubt it. I imagine they'll view it as something of a waste," Baljeet replied.

At this, Ron flashed with anger, "Then why are you working here anyways? If you think it is such a waste?"

"Well, quite frankly, it was the only place that was hiring computer engineers."

"Then, Mr. Engineer," Ron answered, "if the market is so sparse for people of your qualifications, I think it best to count your blessings and shut your mouth."

Baljeet was just about to issue a witty retort; he'd been waiting for this moment for so long. But, his first word was drowned out by an alarm.

BEEP. BEEP. BEEP.

The speakers blared and a red light flashed near the sprinklers.

"What is that?" Ron shouted. "Did a time jump happen on one of the vacations?"

"No," Baljeet responded, "The Johnson family was the last trip for the next couple days. We have maintenance scheduled for the weekend."

"Then something is going on in the building," Ron screamed over the alarm as he looked to the lights above.

If he'd looked over at Baljeet, he would have seen something of a satisfied smirk replace the expression of frustration on his face with each sound of the alarm. As Ron made his way over to the computer system, a group of large men in full SWAT regalia, guns and all, barged into the room. They trained those guns right at both Ron and Baljeet.

"What the hell?" Ron said.

From behind the front guards, a commander who moved with all the precision of years of military work stepped forward, "Are you Ron Hess, CEO of Time Vacation?"

"I am. Who the devil are you?"

"We are the men that are taking your company over, Mr. Hess."

"What?"

"We are in," the commander leaned into his left shoulder and spoke into a radio system, "Cut the alarms."

A second later, the beeping stopped. The commander looked towards Ron Hess and explained, "For a short period of time, of course. But, you heard me correctly. We are taking this place over."

"You can't do that!" Ron said urgently. "There are lock downs, backup measures, security elements in place so that you can never bypass the system. You wouldn't be able to navigate inside anyways. And, we still have people in there. They'll die if you screw things up."

"We've pulled all of your people out," the commander responded. "It's just you two left."

"Well," Ron answered, "my point stands. You will never bypass the security systems that we have between us. And you wouldn't know what to do once you did."

"Yes, they will," Baljeet said quietly towards his former boss. As he did so, Baljeet walked towards the military commander and handed them a thick red security card, "That has all the bypass mechanisms you will need. There is one more numerical password, which I have memorized. Of course, I'll guide you all through."

"What are you doing Baljeet? You can't!"

"Spare me the pleas and attempts at guilt, Ronald. They made me a better offer than you ever did."

"Who did?"

"I did."

Ron turned around to see one of his least favorite people in the entire world stride through the door of *his business'* control center. Behind him walked Brad Hammer and Dennis Fast, who were guiding a blindfolded attractive brunette in jean shorts and a tank top, both tight enough to make a priest look twice.

He snarled furiously, "Dale Brooks. What the hell are you doing here?"

"I think you have an idea, Ron. I have an investment, and I'm going to make sure that investment pays off."

"Dale, I told you that this system cannot be used the way you want to use it. You have no idea what you are doing. You could destroy everything. And, it isn't just my livelihood at stake. This is bigger than you or me."

"Nonsense Ron, you can live your life in the shadow of fear. I'm going to take a few risks and see what the world will give me for my efforts."

"You'll never get away with this."

"Look around you Ron. I already have," Dale said slyly. He then looked towards the guards, "Take him away."

They grabbed Ron roughly by his arms and led him out of the room. Once they'd left, Dale turned to Baljeet, "Is everything ready for our entrance?"

"Just give me a minute," Baljeet said, as he turned towards the central monitors.

As he typed and worked the keyboard, he asked, "Who is she? And, is she going too? I'll need to pull a pod for her."

"This is our expert," Dale said, motioning to Dennis to take off her blindfold.

"I don't see why that was necessary," Becca said as her eyes were uncovered. "And, what the heck is going on here anyways?"

As she looked around, she gasped, "Holy shit. I know this room. Those pods. I've seen the commercials. This is Time Vacation. What in the world…" She looked towards Dale.

"Well, I said we needed an expert. And, that you could lounge on ships all day. I just didn't say what year you'd be doing the lounging." He paused, noticing the angry flash of deceit in her eyes, "Calm down Baxter! Think of the books you can write once this is over. What better way to be an expert on a time period than to actually visit it!"

"No." She replied, "No. No, no, no, no, no. I can't do it. I have to get out of here," she said urgently and made her move towards the door.

"That isn't going to work for us, Becca," Dale said somewhat maliciously, motioning to the guards to stop her.

Those guards walked in front of the door, blocking it entirely, and Dale pulled his own gun out of his jacket. He walked over to Becca, ran the barrel of the pistol gently down the side of her face, tracing her jawline from temple to chin. She shuddered as he did so, and seemed to relinquish any notion of escaping.

Then, with all of the calm and darkness of a Bond-villain, he said, "You are coming with us. You are going to help us find those ships. We need your expertise. And, you are perfectly free to enjoy yourself all the while." He paused almost gently, before continuing, "Now quit whining and go stand next to the pod Baljeet has so graciously retrieved for you. If we have any more difficulties, I might rethink the necessity of bringing you along."

She made her way to the pod that the smaller Indian man pointed her. Then, Baljeet handed her, Dale, Dennis, and Brad identical small, clear, glass bottles. They were each marked "Pre-Travel," on an unassuming white label and were approximately the size of an airplane bottle of liquor.

"What is this?" Brad asked.

"It is our standard pre-travel mixture. The explanation is complicated. But, essentially, it contains the mixture needed for your body to travel across time. Plus, it tastes like Sprite! Lemon-lime and carbonation too."

"Okay," Dale said.

The men drank. Dale held up his gun with a wry smile, "Becca, join us will you?" Baljeet pulled out a tablet computer as Becca downed her bottle.

"Everyone in the pods," Baljeet ordered, "I'll control the system with this," he grabbed an iPad. "I can get us back remotely with this. I've left instructions for those who are staying here. You understand what I've told you?" he asked the commander.

"Yes," the commander turned towards Dale. "What do you want us to do with those folks from the company pods? Ron Hess? The Johnson's?"

"I don't have any need for them now. Let them go. Just make sure you keep the building secure. No one, especially Hess, should be allowed in here."

Chapter 7

For Dale and Baljeet, the routine to come was so familiar that it was hardly discernable. Only Becca noticed the pop about three seconds after those doors closed. To her, the sudden and distinct feeling of movement was disconcerting and strange. It was hard to describe, though, because that feeling was accompanied by a simultaneous sensation of stillness. It was like the moment of liftoff in an airplane, such were their bodies pushed backwards. But, that push felt like it was coming and going in every direction. So, it wasn't like she was on one particular course. It certainly wasn't like any sort of travel she'd previously experienced.

After what felt like ages, but was actually just ten seconds, her door opened. She found herself standing in a dark alley. As she peered out of her pod, she saw the others emerging from their own individual travel devices. Down their sun-deprived nook, she saw a bustling street of full daylight. Along it walked darker skinned folks in skirts and cottons of brilliant reds, yellows, and greens. Many of them had their hair in braids, and most were barefoot. Many carried large baskets on top their heads.

"August 20th, 1621," Baljeet announced to the group as he glanced down at his electronic tablet for confirmation. "Welcome to the past."

"Feels like home," Dennis said somewhat ironically.

"Let's go folks." Dale led them down the darkened side street and out into the light. When they came into the full light, Becca gaped in astonishment. The street, to the right, wound down from a slightly elevated hill to a bustling port. She was thrilled at this sight, which she'd studied in so many dusty and dim libraries, come to life. At the same time, she maintained consciousness of the scene they were all creating. More specifically, the scene she was creating. The men with whom she'd arrived were all dressed in time-appropriate garb. Their four new faces, though whiter than the average local's, were hardly worth noticing in this port town. In their haste or disregard for detail, those men had neglected to bring a dress for their female companion. As it was, Becca wore clothes that wouldn't be popularized for women for another 400 years. She would have gotten second looks had she gone back to the 1920s in New York City. But a woman in tight jean shorts and a low cut tank could practically have caused a riot in this part of history.

"Guys," Becca said cautiously as they walked down that that street towards the water. She couldn't decide whether she should follow these men or dash back to the ally in which they'd all arrived. She knew that she couldn't keep walking down *this* street in *these* clothes.

"They have to be here. Somewhere..." Dennis said, ignoring Becca.

She caught traces of Spanish as they walked past one street corner. She remembered enough to recognize the numbers being bandied about by the merchants. Aside from those exceptions, most people spoke to each other in a distinctly British accent.

"I don't see them," he continued, "Or, I don't see enough of them," Dennis said.

"Yeah." Brad answered, "I thought we were looking for hundreds of ships. The logs said that the fleet was huge. I only see five ships here. Or five vessels big enough to cross the ocean."

"They'd better be here. Or soon," Dale answered. "We've searched for too long for these damn things."

"Guys, listen…" Becca started, this time with a more urgent edge to her voice.

Dale just continued talking, "I thought that the new mapping software we developed to track underwater topography was going to do it. But, this is pretty much my last great idea."

"Guys!" Becca screamed and every one of them turned around, along with a few strangers. Then, she dropped her complaints in interest, "What are we doing here?"

"We are here to find those ships."

"Ships?"

"Yeah," Dale answered. "Those ships I told you about in that ritzy hotel bar. We are going to hitch a ride as they head back to England, bearing with them all the jewels and wealth from this pillaged and abundant land. Then, right before they sink, we'll head back to the Time Vacation building. That way, we will know where to search in the modern world. With that knowledge in hand, we will be rich beyond our wildest dreams."

"That is the most far-fetched plan…" Becca started before stopping herself, "and by the way, do you see the way everyone is looking at me? You should have included a period-appropriate dress in your master plan great idea."

"Stay behind me," Dennis answered, "And try not to attract attention. We have something for you back at the house, I think."

"Meanwhile, these people are going to think I'm a witch."

"Or a hooker," Dale laughed.

She ignored the dig at her clothing, and chose not to mention that her wardrobe problems were their fault, "The house?"

"We rented a place!" Dale said enthusiastically, before adding a bit more reluctantly, "We may be here a while. There is a chance we didn't have the exact date."

Baljeet turned to his new companions, "Come on, I'll show you the new lodging for our time here. Ms. Baxter, as to your last question, there are several outfits there I think you might suitable."

They turned away from the harbor towards the left, making their way up a cobblestoned street littered with horse manure. The streets quickly went from bustling and energetic to quiet, and Becca turned to look back at the busy harbor.

"I don't like this," she said.

"You don't like this?" Dale replied caustically. "A true academic. Always wants to study stuff. Never wants to live it. Would you be more comfortable in a stuffy library with dusty books? Is that your idea of living history?"

"No," she answered, "this place is amazing. These details, the reds of the walls, the lilies, the way those white sails are flapping in the breeze, it is all so beautiful. I've never seen more beauty. But, I don't like this plan. You just have no idea all the things that could go wrong."

"Humph." Baljeet grunted dismissively as he glanced over his shoulder at this woman that he'd just met. She was a sharp one. At least she understood the complexity of what he'd pulled off.

He led them further up a subtle incline, took another turn after passing a sort of community courtyard area, until they all finally came to a quaint and friendly looking house surrounded by greenery.

"Here we are," Baljeet announced.

"It's about time!" Dennis groaned, a bit more winded than the others. His beard made him hotter in this climate than he liked.

"Alright," Dale said, "everyone get themselves situated, and then we'll meet back here in the common area for a group discussion and to lay down some ground rules."

"Becca," Baljeet led her to the opposite side of the house as the men, "I thought this might be best for you. A bit of privacy."

"Thank you," she said gratefully, glancing at this assistant who seemed more thoughtful than the rest of these men combined.

As everyone returned to the common area, the mood was festive. They'd found a couple bottles of red wine and opened them,

"Baljeet here thought of everything!" Dale said as he poured himself a glass. "Thankfully, the fact that the British now control these islands does not mean you can't still get some decent Spanish Rioja."

Everyone got a glass, and Dale continued, "That initial walk-through town was a rarity we won't be enjoying frequently. We will try to keep interaction to a minimum. Baljeet has been seen around here a good bit already. So, he will be tasked with re-supplying us."

"Re-supply?" Becca asked. "The kitchen has food for months. How long do you think we are going to be here?"

"As long as it takes," Brad spoke demonstrably in reply.

"According to the logs we have, there is a five year window during which the ships could have departed."

"Five years!" exclaimed Becca, coughing on her wine in surprise. "You all are going to coop me up in this house for five years? What about our lives back home? People will wonder where I am. My family will think I've died. What about my career?"

"The time travel thing does not work like that," Baljeet answered. "Time here does not equal time there. And don't worry, we think we traced it back to some time this year. They'll be here. My guess is that they'll be here soon."

"I agree, Baljeet," answered Brad, "But I'm just confused about the lack of numbers in that harbor. That log spoke of a 100-ship fleet of three mast ships."

"And you are worried that you only saw five down in the port?"

"More than that, I'm worried that the port looks half full with just five smallish ships in it. How is that water going to handle so many? What do you think Dennis?"

"I think that, I've been thinking about nothing else really. Maybe they only brought a few ships in at a time. We have the logs. We know they came through here. Maybe they did the primary loading somewhere else, and just stopped here to resupply before the crossing."

"No single port town in the Caribbean," Becca said angrily, "would have been able to supply a fleet of 100 ships at one time. Those ships would come in staggered, and the logistics coordinator of the whole enterprise would have set it up so that they didn't all need the same things on resupply. That way, you don't have 100 ships that all need cornmeal. Instead, you have 20 that need cornmeal, 20 that need tack, and 20 that need wine. You'll know that they are part of the same fleet by the secondary flags they are flying. They'll all have the Union Jack flying at the height of their masts."

"Union Jack?" Brad interrupted.

"The British flag!" Becca shot back as she glared at Dale. "These are the people you trust to navigate this time period? He doesn't know that kind of thing? You're just brutes out for money. No capacity for thought. "

"Screw you!" Brad glared.

"You were saying, with the flags, Becca," Dale said calmly, totally ignoring the outrage of his colleague.

Becca took a deep breath and continued, "That one will be on top of the mast. But the second flag will tell you what fleet they are a part of."

"And that," Dale gleamed proudly, "is why we brought you along. Good girl!"

"Whatever," Becca stormed out before muttering over her shoulder, "Might as well get some sun if I'm in the Caribbean."

She slammed the back door as she left, but the men could see that she was only going to the porch area. There, she took off her tank top and shorts to reveal the pink and black bikini she'd been wearing underneath. Becca spread herself out on the ground, ready to soak up some sun and forget about the mess she was in.

"Whew!" Brad whistled. "Damn good looking. Funny she was wearing that for the trip."

"I told her to be ready for lounging in the sun the second we arrived." Dale smiled. "I said we wouldn't really need her for a couple days; we would be coordinating everything." Dale smiled a lustful smile, "want me to tell her to cover up?"

"Not at all!"

"Sure it's nice to look at," Brad said, "But what about that attitude. We can't afford to get reckless and angry here. And what if someone sees her out there? People don't suntan here, during this age. They valued pale skin above all else."

"She'll be fine. She just needs a bit of time to cool off. Try not to make her mad, will you Brad? By the way, no one can see in to the back yard area," Dennis reassured his companion.

"A quick rule though," Dale said. "Becca is off limits. She is here for guidance and information only. We don't need to piss her off further by having someone trying lame pickup attempts on her...okay Dennis?"

"Once we get this treasure we'll never have to worry about working to get a dame anyway. First thing's first."

"So, now it's the waiting game?" Brad asked.

"Yeah, but in this game," Dale said slyly, "the winner becomes a billionaire."

"My kind of game," Brad said as he smiled.

Chapter 8

The FBI building was like something out of a crime movie. There were old wooden desks in a great room, at which men and women sat looking at laptops, talking on phones, or rustling through intimidating stacks of papers. Around those desks, people seemed to be hustling wherever they were going. Some of them may have just been heading to the bathroom, but they were moving with a look on their faces that suggested more important business. The entire place smelled of burnt coffee, and most everyone there walked around with a small Styrofoam cup.

In an office down the south hall from that main room, conversations had started tense and had grown downright hostile.

"I warned you before that we needed additional protection."

"And we here at the Bureau had warned you of the grave risks your business model involved."

"I knew the risks," Ron shot back, "and so did you. After all, you helped me with the security systems. What I wonder about right now is, do those systems seem sufficient in hindsight? I asked for more. But, these two," and he pointed dismissively at Agents Rix and Black, "strutted around Time Vacation, talked boldly of protocols, and told me that they'd designed a foolproof system.

Bottom line: the famed FBI's security measures failed. And, the consequences could very well be dire."

"Well, I think we can all agree that we've got more to worry about right now than who is to blame," Agent Harris said with a mixture of diplomacy and apology.

"I think the issue of blame is worth discussion. At least at some point. Especially given then amount of money that was spent. But, on having more to worry about," Ron answered, "I do agree."

"Good," Agent Harris said.

"I don't even know where to start," Ron said.

"Well," Agent Harris said, "we have to get them out of there. So, let's start with that end-goal in mind. While those men are in the system, they could change things, alter the entire course of history."

"And," Ron answered, "Baljeet knows his way around the system. But, he isn't a historian. Without an advisor, it will be harder for them to avoid making mistakes. Even if they did care enough to avoid making them."

"Just so we are clear, and so I can report it to my superiors, what kind of problems could they cause?" Agent Harris asked.

"Hard to say," Ron replied. "We've made our little errors. There was a family one time whose kid snuck an iPhone in to the past, and we believe that the locals saw it very briefly. On one occasion, a client snuck off and got drunk in a pub. When we finally found them, he was telling stories about landing on the moon and television sets. But, the locals at that bar were just as drunk...so we don't think the damage was grave. Bottom line, we've found that time somehow corrects itself after smaller disturbances. The course of history is generally a forgiving thing."

"So, you've never had what you would call a disaster in the system?" Harris asked.

"True. We've never seen that so-called butterfly effect, where small changes create huge consequences. But, you have to remember; we were trying to avoid those small changes. I have no idea what will happen with someone as crass and ill-informed as Dale Brooks stumbling around time periods he does not understand. The course of history may be forgiving, but it's not 'Sermon on the Mount' forgiving."

"Let's hope Dale is more cautious than normal," Harris answered.

"Doubt it," Ron continued, unwilling to subscribe to Harris' unfounded optimism. "The other logistical issue we face is that we are not really sure where they have gone."

"Well, we think we can help on that front. This combination, Dale Brooks, Brad Hammer, and Dennis Fast, were working on something that should help us narrow our focus. We have kept a loose eye on them, and that seems to have been a wise course of action."

"Well, I'm glad to know that you have some leads," Ron said. "I vaguely recognized that girl they brought in blindfolded. Her legs are something that love songs are written about, but, I can't place her."

"We've got the agency's full power working on identifying her. We are utilizing cameras from businesses located near Time Vacation, ATM Cameras, etc. Once we get an accurate facial profile, we'll run her through all kinds of facial recognition software. If she's gotten a driver's license in the last ten years, we'll figure out who she is."

"What do we do until then?" Ron asked.

"There is someone I want you to meet."

"Who?"

"Bring her in, " Harris said to the guard standing by the door.

The guard turned, exited the room, and Ron sat quietly awaiting this mystery woman. When the door opened again, trailing the guard was a stunning woman. She looked to be in her early 30s, had facial structured that suggested Mediterranean ancestry. Fierce cheekbones tracked down to lips that looked like something out of a Cover Girl advertisement. Ron knew that he'd seen this woman before, but when she was much less dolled up.

"This is Rachel Austin," Agent Harris said, "I think she can be of some assistance."

"Have I met you before?" Ron asked.

"In various outfits and costumes," She replied, "I've been watching Time Vacation from near and far for years now."

"Have you taken vacations with us?"

"Yes. To medieval Europe. One to Revolutionary France. Several others."

"I knew I'd seen you before. Why so many trips?"

"Well, we only have one option. I took those trips as tests."

"Huh?" Ron asked surprised.

"I wanted to gain familiarity with the system."

"Well, I'm as familiar with it as anyone alive, and I don't know what our options are in this case," Ron admitted dejectedly.

"That is because you aren't thinking of all the possibilities. I have an outsider's expertise."

"Not sure I'm following you, Ms. Austin."

"We have to go in and bring them back."

"Are you out of your mind? We don't know where we are going. And, we don't know what we will find when we get there. It doesn't work like you suggest. We can't just send a bunch of modern day people in there as a search party."

"There are ways to figure that out, but you have to do some things you are not going to want to do."

"What are those?" asked Ron.

"You are going to have to shut Time Vacation down."

"Never!"

"Well," snapped Agent Harris, "if you won't, we will."

"You can't shut us down."

"The word us doesn't necessarily apply anymore," Harris answered. "And we will. You know we will."

"There is one more thing you'll like even less. We need to contact someone," Rachel continued.

Ron rolled his eyes and rubbed his eyes like someone who is just tired, "I know who you'll try to find. It is the same person I'd look for if I were to attempt something this crazy. And, I don't know where to find him."

Rachel disagreed, "He isn't the hardest person to find, so long as you keep an eye peeled. Gather a team of your most trusted people. We have a plane fueling up. It will take us to see him."

"Look," Ron replied, "finding him isn't the only problem. Convincing him is a whole other matter. He isn't someone that changes his mind lightly. Even if we find him, I have no doubt he'll refuse to come along with us."

"He doesn't have a choice, Ron," Agent Harris replied.

"But," Rachel said, "we want him to come along and cooperate. You've got a few hours until we reach him. I'd suggest, Ron, that you spend those hours thinking about the best ways to break through to him."

"You all don't know him like I know him," Ron argued.

"You must not understand, Mr. Hess," Agent Harris replied. "I don't care about personal connections. I care about the job we need to do. There are no ifs or buts. Follow Ms. Austin and figure it out!"

Chapter 9

The flight was a short one. Ron spent it ruminating about all the past slights and disagreements he knew well would come out as he tried to convince this man to help him. As he tallied up all the grievances, he knew that he really didn't have much ground to stand on. His feelings swung back and forth from guilty to justification. As the small jet started its decent over that beautiful coast, Ron was no closer to having chosen a method of persuasion than when they took off.

Two Lincoln town cars with tinted windows met them at the airport. Ron and Rachel got into one, the others rode behind. The drive took them along windy roads, through a quaint little town with a cute little main street, and then up into some hills that overlooked that town. Blacktop road turned into gravel, until finally they turned off onto what seemed to be nothing more than a mowed pathway. It was a pretty little trail. Overhead, a canopy of trees barely allowed the warmth of the sun to shine through to the network of pretty yellow flowers on the ground.

Pretty place, thought Ron. *Not surprising that he moved away from everything and out to the middle of nowhere, though.*

But, as they pulled up, he saw a quaint little cottage near the edge of a picturesque, small lake. The cottage was well kept, but humble. It couldn't have had more than two bedrooms.

"This is the place?" Ron asked.

"This is it."

"But, this guy is a multi-millionaire. This is a pretty area, but that cabin there barely seems less luxurious than roughing it. He loves to fish, but he also likes the finer things in life. I don't know that this place is his style."

Rachel was positive. "This is his only address. If he had more property or lived somewhere else, we'd know it."

"I trust you. Just don't understand is all. I'm probably stalling a bit, too, if I'm honest."

"Let's get this moving. Time is of the essence."

"I always like it when people use quotes like that around a guy who runs a time travel company."

"You used to run that company, Ron," Rachel reminded him firmly. "It is now occupied by many large men carrying large guns. So, I'd get moving if I were you, if you want it back anytime soon."

Ron opened his car door, stepped out, and shut it gently enough to avoid a loud noise. He was sure they'd been heard driving up, but he saw no need to disturb the peace and quiet out here. Rachel followed behind him at some distance. He approached a red door that stood in sharp contrast to the white clapboard house with navy shutters. The roof was covered in old-fashioned shake shingles, which made this North Carolina cottage look like something out of the lake-district in England.

There was no doorbell, no brass knocker, so Ron rapped firmly on the door. He paused for what he thought long enough, then rapped more loudly. Nothing. There was a relatively new pick-up beside the house, and the yard was well kept and recently mown. If no one was here, they were probably close by. So, he walked around the back of the house into an equally well-manicured back yard. The grass led down to a weathered dock and tin-roofed awning designed to house a small boat. Out in the lake, Ron saw a man in a canoe. Every minute or so, that man would raise his right hand over his head. Ron could see a long but thin rod, and could barely make out the line as he flew backwards, paused, then turned elegantly forward. Before hovering briefly over the surface, the entire line and the attached fly landed softly on the lake. *10-2*, Ron heard his father's voice as he watched. Bring it back to 10 o'clock at the beginning of the cast, then forward and stop at 2 o'clock.

Ron called out towards the man, who turned in response to the noise. He made no hurried movements in response to the visitor, and took a few minutes before starting to paddle his canoe back towards the dock. If it were possible, he conveyed bitterness about being disturbed from his peace. Ron walked down through the back yard, across the little gangplank bridge, and onto the dock. Rachel stayed up by the house, shielded from the fisherman's view by a thick hedge.

The fisherman was dressed for his task. His long and lanky frame was draped in khaki pants and a button up shirt, the kind with plenty of pockets for lures and gear. He'd fished in the distance, and rowed his canoe, with a sense of calm; like someone who did not have to hurry to drink deeply from life's richness. As he got closer to the dock, his face wore an expression of slight frustration for having been called off the lake. That expression contorted to something much worse as the fuzzy figure waving to him from the dock grew more and more clearly someone he hated. By the time he climbed up onto creaky boards, he looked just plain mad.

He took off his wide brimmed hat, wiped his face, and snarled, "Why in the hell are *you here*?"

Ron ignored the greeting. Trying to remain upbeat, he exclaimed, "Maximilian Blank, just the man I needed to see."

"Well, you came out here to the middle of nowhere. I'm guessing you aren't surprised by this turn of good fortune. Save us both some time, and leave, Ron."

"Please Max, hear me out. This is important."

"I doubt that it is important enough for you to interrupt me in the midst of some really good fishing. You know how hard it is to get good fishing this late in the season? And, might I say that what is important to you hardly matters to me."

Again, Ron pressed forward, "Max, I mean it. A group has taken over Time Vacation."

"Hah!" Max laughed maliciously. "My how karma does seem to work her magic. Now you know how it feels."

"They've sent a crew back in time, and we have no way of knowing what sort of damage they are going to inflict upon both past and present."

"That is absolutely not my problem," Max said contemptuously.

"I'd think that some of it is Max, as you remain the primary owner of Time Vacation."

"An owner with no control, no say," he paused. "Thanks to you. And I'd prefer that ownership to be over."

"This could be the end of the company, Max."

"Good. Ten years too late I say. Should have been shut down long ago."

"Look Max. I know that we've got our baggage. But, we don't have to let more people die in the past."

"How dare you! They knew the risks going in. And I don't like to be included in your plural pronoun. There is no *we.*"

"Please, Max. Is there anything I can offer you?" As Ron said it, he knew just how ridiculous that question was. He had nothing that Max could want. Or, nothing that he'd also be willing to give up.

"No."

"Okay, I told them it would be this way."

Max didn't take the bait. He didn't care who *they* were nearly so much as he wanted this talk to be over. Ron looked out over the lake and sighed deeply.

"Max. You are worth tens of millions. Maybe hundreds of millions depending on the climate in the stock market. Shouldn't

81

you be in a mansion? With a proper boat? Even the fishing here…you know they make fish bigger than this out in the big sea? Have you ever been out to the Gulf in April? The speckled trout are magnificent."

"There it is," Max answered. "Ron boiled down to one glib monologue. Everything is always about bigger or grander with you. More. More. More." He looked rather contemptuously at Ron and continued, "This is all I need. A roof over my head. All the hunting and fishing I need. A bookshelf full of good reads. A snifter of Brandy. No one to bother me. This is all I could ask for."

"But still…"

"Everything I need," Max interrupted.

At that, Ron turned slowly to leave and Max watched him. Both men noticed at the same time that Rachel had left her hiding spot and was walking down towards them.

"Whew!" Max whistled threw his teeth. "Almost everything."

At the presence of a beautiful lady, Max' angry expression immediately gave way to something else. "Ron, you son of a bitch," he said almost darkly but with mock cheer, "the company you keep has improved."

"Hello," he reached out his hand to greet Rachel as she walked down, "I am Maximilian Blank."

"Rachel Austin, Mr. Blank. Pleased to meet you."

"I assure you, Ms. Austin, the pleasure is all mine." As he said it, Max looked Rachel up and down, taking special interest in the curves of her tight skirt.

"Ron," She turned away from Max, "I just got off the phone, and we've received a bit of information."

"You get service out here?" Max joked.

"The organization I work for does not use normal phones," Rachel answered tartly.

"Organization?"

Rachel ignored him, "Anyway, the people who went in— Dale Brooks, Dennis Fast, Brad Hammer, and Baljeet—we knew about."

"Baljeet still working there?" Max laughed.

"Not anymore," Ron answered somewhat glumly.

"That woman that was taken in with them, the one no one could place..."

"Yeah," Ron prodded.

"Her name is Becca Baxter."

At that news, Max dropped his attempt at charming and nearly shouted, "You let Becca go in there? You stupid, ignorant..."

He charged full force towards Ron, tackled him, slammed his upper body down on the ground, and readied a punch. Ron tried to cover his face, Rachel watched with interest, but Max caught himself before swinging.

"Damn you and your stupid company. Damn this time travel all to hell. I should kill you right now for this Ron, but I won't in front of her. Not in front of a woman."

At that, he picked himself up and walked away. Ron straightened his shirt, as if attempting to repair his wounded pride. Getting tackled and whipped in front of Rachel was not the best thing for his ego. But, he now had what he'd previously lacked: leverage.

"Look," Ron said, "I didn't know that was her. But, now this is even more reason for you to…"

"Shut up!" Max shouted. "This is my plan now, and it's a rescue mission. We get Becca out. The rest can die, find what they are looking for, or jump into a black hole for all I care, but we get Becca out."

"Good," Rachel said. "We're glad you'll be helping."

"Listen, sweetheart, let's be clear right up front. You'll be helping. I'm running this show now. Come with me."

They made their way towards the cottage to start devising a plan.

Chapter 10

"In here," Max said tersely.

"I'll go get the others," Rachel volunteered.

"Others?"

"Yeah, we brought a team," said Ron. "Quest, Eco, and Zone are out front in another car."

At this news, Max stopped, "Go ahead. We'll wait for you outside."

"They are the best workers the company has," Ron said trying to make conversation.

"I don't know Quest and Eco," Max said, "and if you are going to insist that your employees go by fake names, I think they might at least chose some that are more humanesque."

"They picked 'em. And, I think their choices have a...romantic and adventurous flair," smiled Ron. "But, if your question is about their qualifications, all three are solid. Quest is a time scientist. Eco is a new hire, but she's a time period expert. Zone, you have met, but he has become a sort of new-age mechanic."

As he described them, the three in question approached. Eco was indeed young. She was spritely too, with short hair spiked and colored extravagantly. Quest, Max noted, looked the part of a runner. Long and lean. Zone, on the other hand, definitely fit his description as the mechanic. He had tattoos on his forearms and wore a goatee. Max shook his hand in greeting.

"Zone."

"Max. Good to see you."

Once they'd all gotten around to the back of the house, and been introduced to Max, he paused a second and looked at everyone.

"Well, here goes." Max opened the door to his basement.

Their conception of this cottage as some sort of rural hideaway was instantly shattered as Max led them into a spotless, gleaming room of stainless steel. Half a dozen time-travel pods flanked the control center, whose graphs and metrics gleamed red and green.

"I knew you had a system somewhere," Ron exclaimed.

"Maybe my choice of address makes a bit more sense to you now, too. I can't afford to risk these things in the middle of a populated area."

"True," said Ron.

"But, of course I have a system," snarled Max. You didn't think my father would leave you to your own devices, did you? He knew a day like this would come."

"I sure wish he'd been wrong," muttered Ron sadly.

"Okay," Max continued, "I'm going to tell each of you this as simply as I can. There is a good chance you will die in there. This is incredibly dangerous."

"How dangerous?" asked Eco slowly.

Max took a breath before he answered, but his anger was still readily evident, "I thought by saying you could die that I was pretty clear. Would it help you if I spelled out some of the ways in which you could meet your end?"

Zone argued some with the fear mongering, "It's just finding some people and getting them out, which shouldn't be too hair raising. We've done this sort of thing before, Max."

"Yeah," Ron said, "But we also have to make sure we aren't drawing any attention to ourselves, not affecting the course of history."

"That is what our jobs are. We've been on plenty of missions," Quest said. "We know what we are doing."

"So, five of us are going back?" Max asked.

"It'll just be you four," Ron said, implicitly recusing himself from the mission.

That subtle statement didn't sneak by his audience. Instead, it earned a fierce reply from Max, "This is your problem and you are damn well going to take responsibility for it, Ron."

"I am not shirking responsibility. But, someone needs to stay back here and monitor things from the present."

"In my world," Max said angrily, "Taking responsibility means getting your ass off the sidelines. Your dumbass got her stuck in the system. You are going to help get her out."

Rachel chimed in matter-of-factly, "The number will be six, actually."

"What?" Quest replied.

"I have to be a part of this. I need to make sure it's done right. And, you need a Bureau presence with you to handle the arrests once you find these people."

"This is not the time for untrained passengers," Max said, looking to Ron for agreement.

"I'd beg to differ, Max. I have my orders."

"From whom?"

"Well," Rachel said, "I'd think the logo on my jacket here might make that clear. The FBI."

Max had never taken orders from the FBI in his life before, and he gave Rachel a look that made clear he wasn't keen on starting. Then, she watched him as what looked like a second set of thoughts flashed behind his eyes. For some reason, he dropped his protestations. Ron took the reins some as Max began to ready the pods.

"We need a plan. Rachel, have we pinpointed the location they went to yet?"

"No."

Max looked up at them and muttered, "No need."

The rest of the group looked perplexed, and Quest—running through all the rules of time science he'd picked up in training—asked the question they all were thinking.

"What do you mean, Max? Of course we need to know where they are."

Max looked like he was thinking of how to explain it. But, then he stopped, "Oh ye of little faith. No need at all. We do not need to know those kinds of specifics. When someone goes back it leaves a time trail. Kind of like Hansel and Gretel leaving bread crumbs in the forest. But, these crumbs stick around; there aren't birds to come and eliminate the evidence."

"I've never heard of this theory."

"That is because you didn't have the teacher that I did."

As he spoke, Max moved to the computer console and began typing rapidly. The others looked on quietly, anticipating that he'd continue his explanation, "By tracking that trail, I can create a time jump."

"A what?" Rachel asked.

"A time jump." Max continued, "It doesn't matter where they are, because I am going to transport them to where I want them to be. The only way you can get back is through a time door. They will not know where the time door is for their new location and we can offer them the chance to go with us or be trapped forever."

Eco responded, "But, we face time jumps all the time and know how to search out the doors. Baljeet will know as well. They will go back to Time Vacation and start over."

"Right," Max nodded as if he had anticipated the question, "That is why we need to do this quickly. I am shutting down their time door, leaving only ours open."

Quest pursed his lips and replied, "But there's a chance they might not be able to get back to the pods at Time Vacation."

"That's why we need to bring them through our doors. Once we have them I can create another time door to jump through."

"It will work that easily?" Rachel asked with a degree of skepticism.

"Make no mistake Rachel, none of this will be easy, least of all finding them before they die where I'm sending them."

"There is one other problem we need to be mindful of." Eco cautioned.

"What's that?" Ron asked.

"Once a singular time jump has happened then the risk of multiple time jumps increases. We could be jumped to another time before we find our door."

Max paused, then nodded. "It is possible, but I have a system, one that my father created, that will allow us to create a door at will."

"Create a door at will? That is impossible. It goes against all of the scientific underpinnings of time travel," Eco said in disbelief. "Who is your father anyway?"

"Daniel Blank. The creator of time travel."

"Max..." Eco said as her wheels churned, "Maximilian. You are Maximilian Blank?"

"The one and only," Max said, bowing theatrically.

The rest of the group laughed some at the naivety of their newest member. They all knew the history of Max and his father. The two were legends of the Time Travel industry. But, that legend also included the subsequent public regret the Blanks had expressed over having invented Time Travel in the first place. Like Alfred Nobel's invention of dynamite, which he regretted so much that he created a prize for global peace, Daniel Blank had come to rue the day he had his epiphany. His son survived him in life and kept that fire of disdain burning.

"I hate this whole system," Max swore under his breath, "and swore I'd never go back again."

"Max, you don't have a choice."

"Don't you think I know that, Ron? I have no choice because of what you did. When you let Becca go back, you practically punched my card too."

"I didn't let Becca go back, Max. I didn't even know who she was, that was all Dale Brooks' doing."

Eco, still new and unaware that she should probably just stay quiet, asked, "Why is she so important to you?"

Max paused. "She isn't to me. Well, she is. It's complicated."

"Does it have something to do with what happened to your Dad?" Eco asked innocently. She could not have been prepared for the anger that greeted that question.

"I don't talk to strangers about my father's death. You certainly have a way of asking too many questions there young'un. If I were you, I'd sit back and be quiet for a bit. See what you learn."

"Sorry," Eco muttered quietly.

"Alright," Max said, turning and looking towards all five of his co-travelers, "Drink up everyone."

He distributed those little clear vials. One by one, each person drank theirs and entered their pod. As the doors closed around the room, Max alone was left standing. He paused, looked around the room, and then turned towards the control panel. He looked like a man torn by an undesirable task and an absolute obligation. His face was a mixture of resignation and resolution. Before stepping into his pod, he looked over at picture of two men, the eldest of whom looked a great deal like Max. The younger was a boy of 12 or 13, grinning from ear to ear and wearing a goofy haircut. Together they were holding a stringer full of bluegills and crappie. The boy was struggling to hold his up, and the father was reaching over his shoulder to offer assistance.

"Father," he muttered like a long lost prayer, "please help us."

Chapter 11

The men sat quietly in their Caribbean dining room. It was indeed a stunning place. They sat and ate shrimp larger than anything they'd ever gotten in the United States, fish caught not six hours earlier, and the bounty from some local's garden. As they peeled their shrimp and nibbled on their corn, they looked out over the bay and the ocean beyond. The crystalline blue seas were capped in white; it was rough out there today. That surf was the result of a stiff south wind that cooled the air in the house. Had they been on a ship, these men might have resented the breeze. Brad for one had struggled mightily with seasickness the first few weeks of their explorations having never been on seas that rocky.

This evening, they relished the breeze and watched from the safety and stillness of land. The novelty of this place had started to subside a bit over the previous weeks. The food was still great, but they were a long ways from home. Where once they'd felt excitement about the promise of riches to come, now they just wondered when something would happen.

"So," Dennis asked Dale, "still no word?"

"Well, there is one lead." Dale answered, trying to drum up a bit of positivity. He continued, "The harbor master tells me that a fleet of ships is attempting to make their way here before the winter. He received that news from an arrival this morning."

"That sounds promising," Brad said.

"Yeah, but..." Dale trailed off.

"But what?"

"Well, a couple things. It isn't a fleet big enough to match the descriptions we have from our travel logs."

"That doesn't mean much," Dennis said, "We knew that the ships that resupply here could be part of a larger combination of fleets. If we find out that they are part of Her Majesty's contingent, it is still likely that by traveling with them we'll find those treasures for which we are searching."

"It's possible," Brad said reluctantly, though his earlier enthusiasm and hopes of promising news had dimmed some.

"This is all your territory," Baljeet said. "I don't know much about this ship business. But, I do know that we've been here longer than I anticipated. As a result, I am starting to worry a great deal about how much we are interacting with the locals. These daily trips to visit with the harbormaster are bound to linger in his memory. I'm starting to look familiar to the fishmongers and vegetable hawkers. We are creating too much of an impression."

"Don't you worry about that," Dale responded testily. "I have plenty of ways to deal with him."

"What are you talking about?" Baljeet asked.

"I have my plans and you have your job," Dale said. "Why don't you worry about what you need to do and leave the rest to me."

Brad intervened, trying to break the tense mood between Baljeet and Dale, "Dale, I'm just a bit worried about the fact that we haven't heard anything about the treasure. We've heard no word about these ships carrying with them anything of value, even the ships that are expected soon. They surely would have been well-secure ships if they were on the sort of mission we think."

"Well, I say that I told you all this would be an exercise in patience."

"I'm pretty patient, Dale," Dennis answered. "But not everyone came here voluntarily. And, it seems like our historian's patience might be wearing a bit thin. We never see her. She never eats with us. What good is a historical advisor that is too pissed off to give us any advice?"

In his tone was the frustration of a man who never gets to see or interact with an attractive woman. But, there were also elements of real concern for the mission. Without Becca, this group would be lost once they got on those ships. They needed to figure out a way to get her on board, literally as well as psychologically.

"Well," Dale said in response, "she is still frustrated with me mostly. I did lie to her to get her here. In retrospect, that might not have been the best plan."

Baljeet spoke with a bit less emotion, "I don't know that you all have noticed, but I don't think she's just angry; she also seems genuinely terrified. Even after we've been here for weeks and seen that things are pretty low key, it's like she's afraid of her own shadow."

Dale nodded, "I get the anger bit. But, the fear is a bit confusing to me as well. I've noticed that she's jumpy too."

"Is she out back again?" Dennis asked.

"I'd assume. She never leaves that deck. At least she'll leave here with a good tan!" Baljeet joked.

"I'll go chat with her." Dennis said.

'No!" Dale interjected. "Let me."

Reluctantly, Dennis deferred to his boss. All of the men watched as Dale made his way through the side hallway and out to the back deck. He emerged onto a deck shrouded in greenery and blooming roses of yellows and reds, from which you could see the port in the distance. But, the beauty of the surroundings was not the first thing that caught his eye in the sun's brilliant light. Becca was. She lay on a reclining chair, which was draped in a sort of cotton cover, reading a book. During her days spent alone on this deck, she had practiced yoga and worked on her tan. Dale thought she'd become even more alluring. Dale had always had a thing for bikini clad women with a tan.

"Becca," Dale started awkwardly.

"You can save your breath, Brooks. I will eat after you all are done. And, before anyone asks me tomorrow, I'll eat alone then too. I have no desire to break bread or share wine with you all."

"You know, honey, it wouldn't hurt to give us a chance."

"Do not call me honey, you ignorant ass! You have no clue, do you?"

"I don't have a clue what you mean," he said jokingly.

96

"No clue why I'm so scared right now."

He was surprised to hear her reference what they'd been talking about minutes earlier. Had she heard them?

"No," he answered.

"Then go back inside and leave me be."

"Look, Becca, I promise you that I'll do anything I can to make this up to you when we get back. Anything you want."

"You don't have what I want," she snapped. "What I want most of all is to be home and living my life."

"Soon enough," he started.

"You keep acting as if you know what you are talking about. Well, I know enough about you to doubt your confidence. I know who you are." She adopted a now sarcastic tone, "The great Dale Brooks. College drop-out who then discovers a shipwreck while working for a salvage company. But, instead of telling your bosses about finding the thing you were supposed to be finding, you cut them out. You went and connected with Brad Hammer and founded your own company. You made your first million on someone else's back."

"That isn't totally fair," Dale replied in a tone that suggested it absolutely was.

Becca continued, "You didn't care about history or allegiances. You didn't care about loyalty or the people who took a chance by hiring you. You just cared about money. Money and fame. Nothing but ego. Your kind of adventurer disgusts me!"

"You don't even know me," Dale meekly argued. He'd have to admit, though, that what she said was pretty accurate. It just didn't sound as bad in his own mind. Fame was not a bad thing.

"I know enough. Any man that takes the risks you've taken on this trip does not care about those around him. The consequences of this stupid expedition could harm generations to come. But, all in the name of money and fame, right Dale? Who cares about the collateral damage?"

"Hey," Dale finally reached his boiling point, "if I were you, I'd do a bit less criticizing right now. I may be an ass. And, I may be a bit callous, but, I am also your only way home."

With a sly smile, Becca looked away from her book at this man who knew so little, "There's very little chance any of us will be going home, Dale. The odds are pretty heavy that we will die here. You just don't know it yet. How would you have any inkling? You have no experience with this business…"

As she spoke, almost as confirmation of the gravity of her words, the pleasant breeze turned much stronger. The trees around them began to sway, smaller limbs began to fall. The gusts of wind came in three rapid bursts. The air adopted an entirely different feel, like the universe had suddenly shifted. The change was both unmistakable and unexplainable. Becca leaned up out of her reclining position and looked around, then nodded.

"What is happening?" Dale asked.

"Time jump," she said plainly.

"Huh? Time jump?"

Instead of explaining, Becca seemed to take some enjoyment from Dale's confusion. "Take a long last look at this bay, Dale, because we are about to go somewhere new entirely. And, in the process we may lose our time door forever."

"What are you talking about?" he said.

"The fact that you don't know what I'm talking about is perfectly illustrative of why you should never have tried this. It might just signify how slim your chances are at survival. And, it is exactly the reason that I've worn an expression of fear since we got here."

Dale looked concerned for just a split second before everything went white.

Chapter 12

The biggest difference between that placid and peaceful scene upon a fishing lake in North Carolina and here was…well, everything. The first thing you noticed, though, was the noise. It was so loud that the air almost felt busy. Indeed, through that air zipped machine gun fire. Through it fell pieces of buildings, crumbling in the percussive impact of bombs dropped from planes overhead. Almost as a soundtrack to all that violent noise, whined the scream of an air raid siren. Ron thought, as he heard that siren, of the small town in which he'd grown up. They'd tested their tornado sirens on the first day of each month. Those tests had lasted a few minutes. He couldn't help but wonder how long these sirens had been screaming. He was darkly certain that they'd been going longer than a few minutes.

Into this war, Max, Ron, Rachel, Quest, Zone, and Eco all suddenly appeared. The violence seemed to be coming from, and happening in, all directions. Most of them were so shocked that they stood frozen and unable to respond. Indeed, if they'd wanted to move in those first few seconds after they arrived, they would hardly have been able to. None of them even knew where to run. None of them, that is, except Max. He was a bit out of practice with these jumps, but got his bearings much more quickly than the others. While they were still catching their breath, Max was calmly and efficiently scanning the horizon. After six seconds, and roughly 1000 machine gun shots, he found what he wanted: a stone structure that looked unoccupied.

"Where the hell are we?" Ron asked.

"I'm not 100 percent sure," Max replied lightly and with little concern, before urgently insisting, "but follow me. We've got to find cover, fast! Or, we won't be here long."

They rushed down the street, trying to stick as close to the edge as possible. By hugging the edges, they were sheltered some by the semi-intact awnings overhead. Any shelter was better than nothing, as machine gunners seemed to have taken a keen interest in their number. All around them, miraculously, bullets skipped and thudded. None hit their marks. As they ran, Eco looked up to see a building nearby, either hit by a falling bomb or finally deciding to give up, starting to collapse. It was like slow motion, sort of like when a city blows up a large building and it hovers for a few seconds weightless before collapsing. As Eco stayed deep in thought, Max led them into the smaller building he'd chosen as their shelter.

When they'd made their way under the entryway, they all ducked through a semi-exploded doorway. When they entered the room, Max breathed a sigh of relief that his choice of structure was unoccupied by any angry soldier or armed civilian. Once they were all inside, they stood with their hands on their knees for a couple seconds, gasping at the exertion of running and coming down—ever so slightly—from the surge of adrenaline that had coursed through their veins.

After about thirty seconds, Max spoke, "We could be any number of places. War isn't necessarily bound by time or geography."

"Do you have a best guess?" Ron asked.

"Maybe a World War II city—in Poland, perhaps?"

"I was thinking Kosovo," Rachel chimed in.

"How the hell can we be somewhere and you not know where it is?" Ron asked with some anger seeping through the fear in his voice.

"The jumps can be like that," Max said calmly. "I wanted a place that was bad. Bad enough so that when they saw people of their time they would come to us, not run. We needed them to need us. If they thought they could locate the door on their own, this whole thing would have been for naught. We'd have lost them. Do you all think this will induce the proper amount of fear?"

"Ha!" they all laughed darkly.

"Okay," Quest said gamely, "what's the plan?"

"We split up. Ron, you lead Quest, Zone, and Eco to find the other group. Search buildings. Hiding spots. Anywhere you would go if you popped into a war zone without warning."

"What will you all be doing?"

"Rachel and I will try to locate the door," he paused. "We have to do that or all is lost anyways."

Rachel looked a bit relieved to have been assigned to the only person who had actually ever done this before. And, she couldn't complain about Max's sense of fearlessness either. She'd heard rumors of his appeal. Now, she could see it with her own eyes.

"How hard will it be to find the door?" Ron asked.

Max responded with an answer that no one understood, "Harder than finding an address, but easier than finding your car keys."

"What?"

Instead of answering, Max continued, "When you've got that group, meet back here. Tell them that if they want to get out of this, they'll come with us. If they don't want to get out of this, tell them they are more than welcome to stick around here and navigate the locals."

At that, he grabbed Rachel's hand and dashed off. Ron looked around at these employees of his in whom he'd had so much faith just days earlier. He could see the doubt in their eyes.

"What do you all think?" he asked.

Eco spoke with a tremor in her voice, "I've been in some bad spots for Time Vacation, but I don't like this one little bit."

"Neither do I," agreed Quest. "And my main problem isn't just with this place; it's also with our guide. There is something he isn't telling us."

"I got that feeling as well."

Zone nodded before he asked, "And where do we even start to look around here? We are in what seems to be a major city. Finding a group of people isn't gonna be the easiest task in the world even in peace-time. But, in this city, we also have to dodge heavy artillery."

"Any of you have any combat training?" Ron asked.

"You are talking to a bunch of scientists and computer nerds," Eco laughed. "The closest thing you are gonna find is experts in *Medieval Fantasy Quest.*"

"Hey," Zone quipped back, "it took me thousands of hours and two girlfriends to reach expert status in that game. I'm quite proud of my achievement, actually!"

"Hmm," Ron huffed, "that is what I was afraid of. Let's stay close and move methodically. We need to be sure we don't get out into the open. Stay close to the buildings and stick together."

"Why couldn't he have picked a nicer place again?" Eco said.

"Because a relaxing beach or leisurely mountain village wouldn't have stopped them," Ron answered. "Follow me."

They made their way out the door and into the city. The roar of guns and bombs had temporarily stopped, but the air was pregnant with the promise of future violence. Ron and the others knew that they'd better move with a purpose. The sooner they could get out of this place, the better.

Chapter 13

Whereas Ron and Max's group had time jumped into the middle of a street busy with gunfire, Dale's group had, luckily, appeared in the lobby of some dusty and blown out building. The walls were all made of thick stone. And the ceilings had seemingly survived what had surely been a thorough bombing. Somehow, even though they'd been in different spots in that Caribbean hideaway, most of the group had appeared together.

"Where the hell are we?" Dale asked.

"From the looks of it," Baljeet answered, "a bank."

"You know what I mean," Dale said.

"Oh, more broadly? Well, looks to be Europe. Eastern, I'd say. And, from the sound of things outside, this country has seen more peaceful days. Unfortunately, that narrows it down to the whole damn continent."

"Guys, look!" Dennis urged his colleagues. He stood looking out what had previously been a glass window onto the street two stories below. A block away from that window, as the others joined him, they all looked out to witness olive green and khaki tanks lumbering down the streets.

"Those are Panzers," Dennis said.

"How do you know that?" Dale said.

"I had a model phase. The Panzer was one of my first big projects. Took me three months."

Brad agreed, "Well, I've never built 'em. But, I've watched enough of the History Channel to agree with you. Nobody's seen *Kelly's Heroes* in this group?"

Everyone was silent, so Brad continued, "Well, if you had, you'd know that those are Panzers for sure. So, that means we've just somehow gone from 1600s Caribbean to 1940s Europe?"

"World War II," Baljeet concurred. "And, since all of the posters around this bank are in German, I'd say we are in either Germany or part of the occupied territories."

"Hey," Brad looked around suddenly, "where is Becca?"

"Shit," Dale answered. "She didn't jump with us?"

"She would have had to," Baljeet answered. As he spoke, each of the members of this team realized how dependent they were on having someone that actually understood what in the world was going on here. "But, she could have ended up somewhere else. Our best bet is to find our own time door, go back to Time Vacation, and use that as a place from which to start searching."

"Find our own time door?" Brad asked.

"Yep. It'll show up as a sort of shimmering square. You all remember the one we got out of?"

"Yes, of course. And that is a good plan," Dale said. "Then, we go back in to the Caribbean, find our ships, and be done with this thing."

"It should be doable," Baljeet said reluctantly.

"Then why is there still fear in your voice?" asked Dale.

"Well, we have to find the damn door. And, whoever has arranged for us to be here knew what he was doing."

"How hard will it be to find the door?" Dennis asked nervously.

"Uh...somewhere between hard and impossible."

"What does that mean, Baljeet?"

"Honestly guys, I'd say we have two options. The first is that we wait here. Often times after a jump, the system senses the error and will bring you a safety door to where you've landed."

"Why is that one of two options? What are the downsides to it?" Dennis continued with his nerves. He was making everyone else a bit more frantic with his questions.

"The downside is just time," Baljeet answered. "That door could appear in five minutes or a week from now. We have no way of knowing when it will come, and we will only have a limited window to access it. When it shows up, if someone is in the bathroom, they could very well fail to make it back in time."

The other guys glanced around nervously at each other. This first option seemed to have a lot of problems. Foremost among those was the fact that it might very well involve living in a war zone for a week, with each day plagued more and more by doubt and anxiety. No one wanted to hold it for two weeks.

Dale said what everyone else was thinking, "And the other option."

"Well, the doors are locational."

"In layman's terms, Baljeet!"

"You all remember the door we entered through in the Caribbean?"

"Of course," they all said.

"Well, that door in the Caribbean was in a location relative to our position here. We just need to figure out the directions and distance, and we can walk through the war zone to find it."

"So," Dale asked, "You are saying that the path we took to get from the door in the Caribbean to our house, if we could track that exact path in this new place, we'd find a door?"

"Precisely," Baljeet replied. "It really is a neat wrinkle in the system. We'll just need to get through a war zone here to find the new door. And, we'd have to figure out how these streets and this topography maps on top of the one we just came from. With the right mathematical approach, it is doable."

The look on everyone's faces, that look of doubt as Baljeet had described waiting for a week for a door to appear, had hardly been resolved by this new option.

"Dennis, what do you think?" asked Brad.

"Hold on," Baljeet said, "there are errors that can occur even with this option. With a jump like we just experienced, the corresponding door might not be active when we arrive. There are no guarantees that, even if we found the right locale, we'd find an operational door."

Dale looked as if that detail had helped him finalize his choice, "Then we wait. We will keep a lookout here. Watch for Becca. Wait for the door to open."

"I don't like waiting," Dennis said. "All due respect, Dale. But, I'd prefer to get out and do something."

"Well, if you do that, you are going into a warzone in a foreign land all by yourself. But, be my guest." Dale replied tersely.

"Uh...I'll stick here with you guys." Dennis caved.

"Then you are first watch. We'll keep an eye on the streets from that window over there and this one here."

They all settled in for what felt like it could be a while. As Dennis and Brad watched their respective windows, the others anxiously watched the doors of the bank. Dale searched around for something to help as a barricade. After all, if the wrong group of German soldiers came into this abandoned bank to find a bunch of strangely dressed guys who only spoke English, time doors would move pretty quickly down the list of priorities. The treasure would be lost forever. And so would their lives.

Chapter 14

The group of travelers made their way along a cobblestone street, past the senseless destruction of war. On some street corners, they were forced to jump over café tables strewn and broken upon the sidewalks, the legs of which had been fractured by indiscriminate bombs. Those tables stood as reminders both of the devastation this town had endured, but also of less violent summer evenings. In the midst of gunfire and raging war, Rachel somehow found those broken tables to be the most depressing. Someone had sat at those tables and enjoyed a nice glass of wine. Some man had waited on his wife to join him for lunch.

No time for much mediation upon that now, though. Each twist and turn brought a new adventure. She didn't know where they were going, but Max seemed to magically know what roads offered detours for the trouble they encountered along the way. Even armed with that knowledge, more than once, they were both forced to duck inside a convenient doorway for cover as a group of people passed. *This luck can't last,* Rachel thought to herself. Sure enough, they were hustling down a long straightaway, and were halfway down the road, when around the corner ahead they saw the front end of a massive army truck making a turn. Rachel and Max turned to look backwards and realized with a sinking feeling, they'd never make it back around the corner before being seen. Instead, they ducked into another of those doorways that presented itself conveniently just to their left.

But this time, the door was locked. They'd need to press up against the side of the entry way and hope that no one in the truck looked back. Even then, they'd be partially visible for a few seconds as it passed. As the truck lumbered closer and closer, and the coughs and sputters of the engine grew louder, Rachel ended up pressed into Maximilian in an effort to hug the wall more closely. The more tightly she clung to Max, the further she'd be from eyesight. Maybe it was the fear and adrenaline. Maybe it was the way he smelled like aftershave and sweat. Whatever it was, Rachel thought to herself in those seconds of danger that parts of the experience weren't all bad. *At least I'm getting to be closer to him.* Just as soon as she'd thought it, the truck was past. Max pushed past her, either unaware of the moment of attraction she'd felt or uninterested in reciprocating it. Whatever he was thinking, they were off again.

Rachel was a runner. She ran the local half marathon every season, and kept up with a 10K every couple months. It was one reason her legs looked the way they did. And, it seemed that Max kept himself in shape too. They'd been moving through the city at a brisk pace, with the occasional stop to hide, for about an hour. In that time, neither had complained or needed a break. Even now, Max showed no signs of slowing. She hated to admit it, competitive fitness freak that she was, but Rachel was starting to get a bit winded. Sweat had been beading up the upper portion of her jaw for a while, and now she realized the back of her shirt was wet. At the very least, she needed to hydrate and stretch soon.

"How much further Max?" she exhaled.

"Just a bit," he answered. He then looked overhead at a noise that sounded indistinguishable to her from the general din all around them.

"Quick!" Max shouted as he pushed her close to a building. He pushed her down onto the ground and leaned over protectively.

"Max! Wha—"

BOOM!

A bomb exploded nearby, and what was left of the windows in houses and businesses on the block crashed down.

"Are you okay?" Max asked as he picked himself up off her and helped her up. He did so with a gentleness that he'd previously not shown her, holding gently onto her arm as he checked on her well-being.

"Yes. How did you know that a bomb was falling?" she asked.

"Humph, I didn't even think about it. I guess you learn to recognize that sound with a bit of practice!"

"Practice?" She said in surprise, "Just how many wars have you been involved in Max?"

"Come on!" he ignored her question and urged her onward, "Just a bit further."

"Where are we going anyways?"

"There is a time door here. A special one that I had ready to go."

"I thought you didn't know where we were going?" Rachel asked playfully.

"I know a bit more than I let on sometimes," he replied. "It helps to have others a step behind."

They ran through a central plaza area, escorted by the shots of a particularly inaccurate sniper, until they were around one last corner.

"We turn here," Max said, before muttering to himself. "Glad I made sure that Becca never came to this horrible place."

"Then why did you bring the others here?" Rachel asked, more than a bit miffed that she hadn't merited the same sense of concern and affection that had obviously led Max to protect Becca.

"I have my reasons. And, you will know them soon enough," Max said not unkindly. But, even this ladies' man misread how much empathy he needed to employ at this moment. Rachel huffed a bit and did not reply as they walked down a darkened street. It looked like a forgotten closet for the city streets, and Rachel grimaced at the stench from the trash bins. Her sense of anger and scorn would have lasted longer, but just ten steps down, Rachel saw something strange. It was a block of light flickering faintly.

"There it is," Max said. "Hurry!"

They rushed through the doorway. Any observers who happened to be watching would have seen a flash of white light as they disappeared, the door vanishing close behind the man and woman almost like it had been waiting for them. For both Rachel and Max, the noise and dusty streets of war were quickly replaced by a dimmer sort of light and slower activity. In an instant, they were standing in the lobby of a fancy hotel. They'd appeared over by the payphones, and somehow no one seemed to have noticed their sudden arrival. *I've got to ask him how we show up and no one ever seems to notice,* Rachel remarked to herself. Now that they were there, they fit right in. Max had somehow transformed into a three-piece black suit. A perfectly pressed white shirt and a light green strip in the tie matched Max's eyes. Rachel had been given by the gods of time travel a tight, sapphire blue dress. *Another question for him: who is picking my wardrobe and how can I hire them for my personal assistants!* These many questions Rachel left in lieu of a more practical one, "How did we get here?"

"No time to explain that now. We'll have plenty of time for conversations about that sort of thing later."

"To go from that place to this one…it seems impossible."

"It is amazing, isn't it?" Max replied. "Let me ask you a question. Can you imagine the past, but in the future?"

"What do you mean?"

"Imagine a moment in time, something that happened to you. Maybe it was grand, maybe it was tragic. But, imagine that it has already happened. The past…imagined in the future."

"Max, are you trying to confuse me?"

"If I was trying to confuse you, I'd use something much less complex."

"Huh?"

"Exactly!"

Max took her by the hand, ignoring her facial expression that begged for a more thorough explanation of everything, and led her through the lobby. In it, she saw people dressed much as she and Max had appeared in this new setting. Everyone looked as if they had just come from an important dinner party or were heading off to some social setting bound to involve paparazzi and celebratory champagne. They were all attractive too, though to some the fates had dealt a particularly gracious hand. They walked by the front desk, and Rachel was surprised to hear one of the workers call Max by name.

"Mr. Blank."

"Hey, Bobby!" Max answered as he strolled past.

Now was not the time to stop and visit. Instead, they made their way down a long hallway, past some open windows into a fitness center, and out towards a pool area. This pool certainly fit the clientele Rachel had noticed in the lobby. Waterfalls of all varieties cascaded down into the main body of water. On one side of the pool, those waterfalls created several smaller pools that steamed with heat. It was like something she'd seen in pictures of the Playboy Mansion. And, the women who emerged from one of those pools, and made their way straight towards them, certainly could have rivaled any of Hugh Hefner's Bunnies in figure and beauty. They were like pin-ups, but these curves were 3D.

Rachel wasn't the kind to get jealous. And, she had enough self-awareness to know that there really was not a ton of reason to be jealous. After all, had she been wearing her bikini, she would have challenged each of these for attention. Competitive, she still felt a subtle pang of anger as the taller one, with black hair and a bikini that matched, walked up and gave Max a kiss on the cheek. The shorter blonde, in a red and yellow bikini that barely covered her upper or lower assets, was next.

"Max, darling!" she cooed as she kissed him on the cheek. Rachel watched this all with a surprised expression, and wondered if this blonde wasn't trying a bit too hard to sound like a glamorous movie starlet.

"Heidi. Lacy. Great to see you, girls." Max answered with a greater degree of cool than most men could have mustered upon being greeted with such enthusiasm by these stunning women.

"You brought a guest, Max?" The darker haired vixen asked.

"A special guest?" asked Heidi, looking for a clue as to who this might be.

"She is a special guest," said Max. "This is Rachel."

"Hello, Rachel," they alternately said as they leaned in and kissed her on the cheek European style. Rachel felt a bit of a shiver as the blonde rested her hand ever so slightly on her shoulder with her kiss.

"Alas, ladies. We are not here for fun. Something has happened. I'm looking for an old friend. Have you seen a woman here?"

"How come all of your friends are women, Max?" asked Heidi playfully.

"She would have been someone you'd never seen before," Max continued.

"No," they answered.

Lacey continued, "We haven't noticed any unusual strangers here lately. And certainly, we haven't seen a strange younger woman. If we had, you know we would have told you."

"I know you would have. But, I wanted to check. If you do see a strange woman, her name is Becca. Stop her. Alert me as soon as possible."

"You've got it, Max," answered Heidi seriously, "You know we'd do more than that for you honey."

Lacey asked, "But are you sure that you and Rachel can't stay a bit?"

Again, Rachel felt those shivers. She knew what the insinuation was and she wasn't entirely used to such things. At the same time, she felt a wave of desire when the ladies offered, "Maybe next time." It was odd to have such feelings. She'd always considered herself—if not politically—to be a bit of a conservative girl. She'd been raised with Midwestern values that had never really left her. Now, in a whole new time and strange place, this feeling? If she'd had the self-awareness to recognize it, Rachel would have identified that her receptivity to a strange adventure was almost entirely based on an ever-intensifying interest in Maximilian Blank.

Chapter 15

Rachel hustled behind Max as he led her back into the hotel and towards that darkened lobby corner where the door had original appeared. She fully expected to be thrust again into a war zone, and was surprised when they stepped through the doorway and emerged onto what seemed to be a quiet Italian street. It seemed to be Renaissance period, judging from the dress. Once again, Rachel was pleased to find herself dressed to the nines. *I love these clothes!* This search for Becca was starting to feel a bit like Halloween. Max didn't turn to explain the unusual locale and Rachel figured she'd just follow quietly. They made their way towards a little café, at which Max stopped and looked around, examining each customer.

"Not here…" he muttered to himself. "Where in the world is she?"

"How many places are we going to visit like this?" Rachel asked.

"As many as it takes."

"How many is that?"

"Well," he paused, "there are lots of places she could be."

"Where are we?" She asked.

"Ah," he smiled, "this is one of my favorites. Why go see Mona Lisa in the Louvre when you can get drunk with Da Vinci on Chianti?"

"Da Vinci is here?"

"He's around somewhere. And, if you poke around enough wine bars, you are sure to find him. Usually too drunk to talk, but sketching away on pieces of paper or the bar-tops anyways."

"Why are you so set on finding this woman?" Rachel asked.

"I have my reasons."

"Were you two lovers?"

First and foremost, he didn't want to answer the question in total. It was just too much to get into at this moment. But, as those words left Rachel's lips, Max knew a few things. He knew by giving more information he'd relinquish some of his carefully cultivated air of mystery. He knew that she wanted him to say no. And, he knew that he had Rachel if he wanted her. In the interim, he dodged.

"Can I answer that question at a later date, please? When I can explain it all to you?"

"And those other women. The Bond girls from the pool? They love you too, Max."

"I'm sure they do Rachel. Though they probably have a different definition of that word than you do."

It was unlike Rachel to get so provocative so quickly with her questions. But, something about this adventure led her to abandon her traditional morals.

"What else do they do, besides swim together?"

"Really? You want to ask that sort of thing? I'm not sure you want to hear the answer. Anyway, we have plenty to do. Let's go."

But, despite his efforts to dodge the question, Rachel persisted, "They seemed so...how do I say this? Different than women I've met before, and I'm not just referencing their looks."

He knew what she meant, but decided to take that question in a slightly different direction,

"Short answer. They are stepsisters. Heidi's dad owns that hotel, among many other things, and they hang out there because they never need to work. They live a life of luxury and, as such, look for adventure where they can find it."

"So, Max, remember when you told me that you sometimes liked to keep some things to yourself? When you ditched the other members of our team back in that war torn scene?"

"Yeah."

"Well, I get the impression that this is sort of like that. Like there is more that you aren't telling me."

Max huffed in frustration. She was really persistent. Maybe it is the investigative component of her job, "One thing I will tell you is that we have got to find Becca. Come on."

And, once again, they were walking down the alleys of that beautiful Italian town. Rachel thought of how much she'd like to come back here with Max sometime. Maybe when they had less to worry about. They stepped into that increasingly familiar doorway, and were once again in a lavish interior space. This time, it seemed to be the bar of a hotel. Rachel looked around astonished. She admired her second glamorous evening gown of the night, and noted that Max seemed to have impeccable taste. Every place they visited, save the war zones, was like something from a movie. In this room of glamorous people, one woman stood out. Rachel didn't recognize her instantly. But her outfit demanded a second look. Others were staring too, but by the look of it, the woman was new to the situation and still getting her bearings. By the time Rachel did make the connection, Max was already on his way in her direction; this was Becca. This was who they'd been looking for.

Becca Baxter was wearing jean shorts and a tank top that really had no place in a fine bar like this. But, she was gorgeous enough to get away with it. Few people will tell a woman who looks like that to leave anywhere, much less a bar.

Rachel hustled up behind to hear Max say urgently, "Becca. Thank God we found you."

In response to this exclamation of thanks, Max was given a swift and serious slap to the face. *Whap!* Max took the response quietly. He held out his hands, palms down, in a gesture of peace. Rachel was confused.

"What was that for?" she asked.

Max and Becca replied simultaneously, "It's a long story."

Max looked at Becca in a way that could only be called deep, but deep in a way that includes mystery, sadness, beauty, and so much more.

Maximillian gently said, "The important thing is that you are safe. I was very worried about you Becca."

"At least someone here cares," Becca sighed. "Where the hell are we?"

"A hotel bar," Max said calmly. "I believe this is The River Grand at The Mantador Hotel."

"Yeah, thanks Captain obvious," Becca scoffed. "The bar, for crying out loud..."

"Okay," said Max, "I don't want to alarm you two too much. I don't think this is one of our normal timeframes."

"What do you mean?"

"It's...this is the future, ladies."

"What!" they both exclaimed.

"Yeah," Max nodded, "I think we are in the future."

Becca thought for a few moments. Rachel looked more than totally confused.

Finally, Becca pursed her lips a bit and said, "But Max. That is impossible. No one has ever been able to go to the future."

"Everyone likes to use the phrase impossible with this stuff. I'm amazed how often I hear that word," Max said. "They seem to forget that the very premise of time travel was 'impossible' until my father figured out how to do it. He invented the system. He hid tons of stuff from pretty much everyone except me. And, I'm sure he hid other stuff even from me. But, he was always able to visit the future. He just made sure no one else could. Too many risks."

"So, what happens here?" Rachel asked. "What do you do in the future?"

"I need some time to think," Max mumbled. "In the meantime, we need to get out of sight. This is way too risky."

But, almost as a direct refutation of that concern, at that same instant, a young bartender dressed in the standard tight black outfit approached them and asked for their drink order. In so doing, though, this lovely barkeep called Max by name, "The usual, Maximillian?"

"Sure." He replied. "Martini's for them."

"Can I get anything else for you all?"

"A room key would be helpful," Max said softly to her.

"Anything for you Maximilian."

The barmaid winked at Max before rushing to the bar. Rachel watched as the barmaid seemed to glow as she talked to the bartender behind the bar, not unsurprisingly, another beautiful blonde woman; athletic, tan, hair from a shampoo commercial, who kept making eyes towards Max. She quickly mixed two Martini's, pulled a bottle of beer from a cooler, opened it, and set all the drinks on a tray. The barmaid rushed back with the order.

"Here you are," she said handing out the drinks. "Good new Max," the barmaid said, reaching into the front of her top, into her bra. She pulled out a key, an old fashioned metal key, and handed it to Max saying, "The penthouse suite is available."

Chapter 16

Eco, Ron, Zone, and Quest were disoriented and scared. They'd been wandering the city now for hours. Still, no sign of the renegade treasure hunters. As they traced street after street, each was plagued by doubt. What would that even do if they found Dale Brooks and the others? Max had been vague, perhaps intentionally vague, but they had no idea what the hell they would even do if they found what they were looking for. How would they find Max again? Without a time door, would they be stuck in this strange place forever? Eco and Quest had seen their share of hairy situations working for Time Vacation, but never before had they been so concerned about their safety and well-being. Both had mothers that would be devastated by their disappearance. Both had things that they were loathed to leave behind. So, naturally, they both began to pepper their boss with questions—questions he would have struggled to answer even if he had been able to clearly hear over the air raid sirens and artillery shelling.

"This is madness, Ron. We shouldn't be here," Eco shouted as they ducked into a building to rest for a second.

"Huh?" Ron asked, rubbing his ears.

"This is madness!"

"Oh," he muttered, now that he could hear a bit better. "Yeah, this place is not going to make our list of options for travel anytime soon."

"You'd at least think that Max—with all his expertise—could have found a better place than this," Quest seconded.

"What if one of these patrols catches us? We've had three narrow misses in the last hour alone. What the hell would they think of us? They would not consider us a friend, I know that much, Ron!"

"Stop your complaining, folks," Ron answered testily. "Max has a reason for this. I trust him."

Zone kicked a rock into a wall, audibly huffed, and said accusingly, "Well, all due respect Ron, but I'm starting to wonder where in the hell all that trust is coming from. Why trust this guy?"

"Why not?" Ron asked.

"This man has wanted to shut Time Vacation down and destroy it ever since his father was killed."

"His efforts," Ron said, "while annoying, have been financial and legal. He wouldn't try to kill anyone. He may be vindictive, but he isn't violent. Are you suggesting he is setting us up here?"

The three others sat quietly for a minute. They all seemed to be on the same page when it came to doubting Max's intentions, but they also seemed to take a step back and think carefully about arguing with their boss.

Zone spoke up, choosing his words wisely, "Ron, he has the CEO of that company trapped in a warzone. He abandoned us with very little explanation of how we'd find him again. Whatever trust you have for him, I think you might need to rethink things here."

"It doesn't look good," Ron conceded, "but I've worked with Max in the past. He is professional. He cares about others. He would not try to kill us, no matter how much he hates the company."

Eco chimed in quietly, "His father is dead, Ron. No one is rational when that sort of stuff happens."

Ron sat quietly for a long while. He looked at the others, saw in them the anxiety and doubt he himself was feeling. He wanted so much to lead them and to assuage those feelings. He had to concede that their logic was entirely reasonable.

"Look, what you all are saying is true. I don't know what the grief Max feels could motivate him to do. We can't know much about his motivations right now, however. There is nothing we can do about those motivations now that we are here, anyway. The only real choice we have is to keep looking for the others. If we happen to see a doorway in the interim, we can discuss that then. On a practical front, what do we know? Where should we go from here?"

Zone sat quietly, seemingly assuaged by the admission of doubt from Ron. Then, he spoke up, "I've been thinking about that. And I'm starting to get this feeling that maybe we're going in circles. Certain stuff is starting to look more and more familiar to me. Like we've been retracing our steps, or like we are in some sort of universe that turns on itself. I don't know how to explain it."

"I've had the same sensation," Ron replied.

"Circles? How is that possible?" Eco said, obviously a bit dismayed at the prospect that their search may have covered less ground than she'd initially thought.

"I'm with Eco," Quest argued. "I don't know how that is possible."

"There are a lot of weird things going on," Zone replied. "How is it that we keep getting these lucky breaks? No one here seems to notice us? I mean, I know we are being careful, but we've wandered for four hours in a war zone and not been seen? We are time travelers, not ninjas."

That last line got a bit of a laugh. The group had to make some decisions. In a compromise of sorts, Quest and Eco agreed that, as they went out to continue their search, they'd try to put a finger on any repetitions they thought they saw. The others agreed to keep plugging away for now and drop the topic. As soon as they'd emerged from their hiding place and walked for perhaps 100 yards, they heard a distant shouting. In a building just within eyesight, a man was screaming and motioning for them to come closer. Somehow, he looked like he didn't belong in this place, though none of the travelers could have articulated what the difference was. Without much of a word, they all made their way in that direction. They ran closely by the wall to reach the bank, rattled by machine gun fire throughout the run.

As they entered what was obviously a bank, they noticed the others standing close by the man who'd motioned. Everyone was covered in dust. They all looked at each other quietly for a minute as Ron leaned over gasping to catch his breath. He was a bit older than his other employees, and was not in their kind of shape. When he finally did look up, hands on his knees, it was to listen to the other group's welcome.

The leader said, "I've a team posted up on the top floor of the building. When they saw you running, unarmed, they told me to motion to you and…" the man stopped what he was saying as Ron looked up. Suddenly, underneath the grime and two-week stubble, he recognized who this was huffing and puffing in front of him.

"Ron?"

"Dale Brooks," Ron curled the last word with disdain. "I told you that your little plan would never work. Did you listen to me? Of course not. Now look at the shit we are all in."

Eco, Zone, and Quest observed the people across from them with a fresh distaste. Brad Hammer, Dennis Fast, and Baljeet returned the favor. Each of the two groups were bound by their common need of each other. It seems that Max's intentions had worked beautifully. In any other universe these two sets of men and women would have torn each other's hair out, but here they needed each other too much to fight.

Max was not here to see his idea achieve success. Nevertheless, these enemies expressed their mutual distaste in body language, but did nothing to enact it. Meanwhile, with this grand plan now fully ruined, Baljeet couldn't help but look upon his old boss Ron with—in addition to all the years of frustration—a healthy dose of humility. He'd messed up big time. And, he knew it. Better than many of the others, he knew it all too well. He also knew that stuff was happening here that was way out of his league. Baljeet had always considered himself underpaid and under-appreciated. Now, he fully realized just how much he hadn't known about time travel compared to Maximilian Blank.

Chapter 17

When they got out to the penthouse, it was impossible to ignore the view. The rounded windows opposite the door made the room feel like something of a bubble. And, the long couches and tables in the room all angled towards those windows. The entire room had been constructed and decorated to draw your eyes towards the city outside. And what a view it was! It was dusk, so Becca and Rachel stood in awe as the city lights, one by one, signaled their readiness for the night to come.

"Beautiful," Rachel said.

"Beautiful indeed," Max replied. But, when she turned, she noticed that he wasn't looking out towards the city so much as towards her legs.

"Hey, Max! Up here." She startled him into looking back up towards her face, "If we are going to go traipsing around in the past, present, and future, dodging bombs and aggressive playmates eager for bedroom time, I'm gonna need to know what is going on between you two. I at least need to understand the dynamics between my travel companions. Why the slap?"

Max gestured to Rachel that she should sit down on the sofa in the middle of the room. After pouring her a glass of red wine from the bottle he'd been opening, he sat across from her on a plush leather chair. They both waited for Becca to turn away from the view, at which point she joined Rachel on the couch. She did not seem eager to explain anything, but instead waited for Max to speak.

"I don't know where to begin," Max paused.

Becca quickly and angrily chimed in, "Let's start with the time you killed my sister."

"What?" Rachel asked in a startled tone. Maybe she'd been wrong about Max after all. Maybe she should work harder to avoid him. He seemed a bit reckless, but she'd not recognized him as any sort of killer.

"I didn't kill anyone," he replied, and Rachel relaxed just a bit.

"That your wife and father died at the same time hardly pardons you. And, I hope you notice I haven't sent any sympathy cards. After all, when you killed your loved ones, you also killed my sister. Sarah just wasn't important to you. My mother and father still haven't recovered. They'll never recover. And every one of those deaths was your fault Max! I knew she never should have married you…"

Max experienced a flash of emotion, equal parts anger and sorrow. He certainly didn't appear to agree with Becca's accusations. But, that expression of disagreement passed as quickly as it appeared. For a few seconds, he just quietly looked towards Becca and raised his hands in the universal gesture of loss and supplication, pursing his lips as if he was thinking how to apologize for an act beyond words, for a deed with consequences that far outran any person's capacity to apologize.

"What happened?" asked Rachel quietly.

"I did not kill my dad or Sarah," Max started, but he said it with such grief in his voice that Becca did not argue. "I loved Sarah with all my heart, Becca. I could not imagine ever loving again after I lost her."

"How did you lose her?" Rachel asked even more quietly.

"Dad, Sarah, and I…we were conducting experiments. Both of them wanted to see what was really possible. I just wanted to please them. They were way ahead of me and my understanding of things. But, we were all pushing the limits of our scientific knowledge and capacity."

Max leaned over in his seat, reached to his back left pocket, and pulled out a wallet. He took out a couple credit and business cards, and then found what he was looking for. It was a tattered little photo.

"This is Sarah."

Sarah quietly took the picture from Max. It showed a much younger Maximilian Blank. He had a thicker head of hair and sported an 80s style mustache. Next to him was a girl that looked to be the spitting image of Becca, with just a few notable differences. The nose was button, just like her sister's, and the forehead high and regal. But, Sarah's brown hair also had a hint of red and her cheeks were slightly sharper than Becca's. The most notable difference was their eyes. Whereas Becca had eyes of light green, out of this picture smiled a girl with the most amazing shade of hazel eyes that Rachel had ever seen.

"Those eyes!" she murmured softly to herself.

Becca nodded knowingly, and Max replied, "They were what got me, originally. They had the tiniest flecks of yellow in them. Somehow, her tan complexion made the brown in her eyes deeper and richer. They were also absolutely fierce and fearless. The things I miss the most about Sarah…they were all in those eyes."

"So, she worked with you from the beginning?"

"Yeah. She was my father's intern. She'd read everything he'd ever written, had looked to him as an intellectual hero of sorts. He turned her request for a job down ten times before she wore him down. By the time this picture was taken, she knew as much about the system as anyone—Dad included."

"Is that Big Ben in the background?"

"It is…" Max said. "We took that picture one day before the accident. We were going to investigate the time jumps…" he trailed off.

Chapter 18

Max, Dan, and Sarah stood in front of the pods waiting for them to properly heat before departure.

When the lights blinked green, and the control board announced robotically, "Go for travel." They stepped into their pods and emerged in exactly the place Max had been aiming for.

"Ladies and gentleman, welcome to the London Bridge. For those of you looking to your calendars, the year is 1882."

"Right on the money my son. Exactly where we wanted to be!" Dan Blank said proudly.

"And the displacement worked perfectly," Sarah added with pride and affection in her voice. "Nice job Max! Are you sure the jump will occur at the right time?"

"Pretty positive," Max said. "I've set it up that way."

"How soon?

"In the next minute or so," Max replied confidently. He then looked towards his computer to start adjusting coordinates. Just as he promised them, one minute later there was a rush of air and a flash of bright light. In an instant, they were in a different place. Or, the same place. Just a different time. It was an odd sensation, and even these time travelers marveled at it. They were in precisely the same spot on London Bridge, but the stone seemed

a slightly different hue. Additionally, one of the bigger buildings lining the river was gone.

"Same spot, as you all can probably tell," Max announced, "but it's one year earlier. London, 1881."

"How many of these will we need to do?" Sarah asked.

"I figured in my calculations," Dan answered authoritatively, "that three fast ones should be adequate."

"Your calculations are usually a pretty good thing to trust," Max replied.

Again, the wind rushed and the light flashed. This time, they stood in the same spot again. This time, however, there were more buildings, not less. And, whereas in that first jump the bricks of the bridge had seemed newer, now they seemed a bit grimier. Like those red bricks had seen just another couple of years' traffic.

"Same spot again. 1885 this time." Max confirmed that they'd moved forward in time a bit.

"Once we get back we can analyze all the data and see if there's a pattern in these time jumps. We need to have this down to a science."

"I agree, Dan," Sarah said. "If there is a pattern, I think we know how to neutralize it."

"That would be the hope," Dan nodded.

Max looked a bit worried as he listened to this portion of the discussion, and voiced one of his many concerns, "We just have to be certain we don't lose our door."

At this warning, Dan shook his head a bit and responded, "I wouldn't worry too much about it, Max. Even if that happened, which is unlikely, I have backups in place."

"Right," Sarah agreed. "The time door you can open at will. Like your own private escape hatch."

Dan Blank appeared almost preoccupied, like he didn't want to have to explain just how thoroughly he'd prepared things, "Yeah, I have it available for just such occasions."

"I still think, Dad, that we should have figured out some other way to do this. It makes me nervous."

"Max," Daniel Blank started, but before he could finish what he was going to say there was another rush of wind and flash of light. In the instant between that sound and the event that followed it, the facial expressions of all three explorers shifted from various degrees of confidence to abject fear and confusion. After the shift, they looked around to find themselves in a completely different city. They were still near water, but now they were looking out over what looked to be a harbor or broad river.

Max looked out to an island in that water. It looked familiar. Something about the shape, and this particular distance, he'd seen countless times. There was a large structure in the center of that island made of concrete bricks. But, it was not a building of any sort. More like a pedestal. Then, it hit him...the Statue of Liberty. They built the pedestal first. Then shipped over the statue from France.

"New York," he said. "We are now in New York City. Same year, 1885."

"But why would it take us someplace else?" Sarah asked.

"That's a good question," Max said as he looked down to his computer tablet and started scrolling through data.

"I think the time jumps are becoming randomized," Dan said, "which is a good thing."

Max was dismayed with how flippant his Dad viewed this very dangerous glitch, "Good thing, Dad? Who knows where we might end up next? You know how unstable this system can become."

"If that happened we could just use by trap door before total collapse happened."

"Maybe, if we knew about the instability before the collapse."

"You worry too much, Max." Sarah tried to reassure Max and compliment her idol at the same time, "This will all work out."

"I have realistic things to worry about, both of you! Each jump makes this system less stable. Now, we are no longer controlling jumps. Who knows—"

A flash of light and whoosh of wind and again they jumped. They stood looking out over Ellis Island, but this time the pedestal was just in its initial stages of construction.

"I think we jumped back a couple years," Dan said.

Much more quickly this time, before they'd had the chance to say anything to each other: Flash! Whoosh!

"Where are we now?" Sarah said, an element of fear now firmly established in the tenor of her voice.

"This is not a city we've been to before," Max said.

"Max, I don't think this is a city that anyone in our time has been to. Judging from the flying cars and futuristic outfits, we have somehow gone forward a couple hundred years."

"We're in the future?" Sarah asked.

"Yes, but it's time to go back," Dan said, then more urgently added, "Now!"

With those words, Dan, Sarah, and Max heard a single crack behind them. They turned to see dust rising up from the ground about 100 yards away. From the looks of it, something had fallen. Then, they noticed something high above the dust shed from the building and gain speed quickly. They watched in horror as a huge stone fell to the ground and exploded loudly. Where people had previously sat at a café, now stood a huge cloud of dust. Worse, that second stone was followed by five more, as the entire side of a building starting shed its skin. Screams from each direction pierced the air. The top leaned over a now unsupported side, and then started to waver towards them. When the travelers turned to look behind them, they saw that this building was not the only one collapsing. Everything was falling down around them.

"This isn't a city that is falling down," Max said, "Time itself is collapsing. This is bad. Really bad."

"Start the evac program!" Dan shouted.

Max worked furiously at his computer, but his fingers were shaking along with his entire body. He couldn't. Hit. The. Right. Keys! Sarah didn't calm him down when she shouted at him to hurry. In what felt like an eternity, finally he clicked through the proper procedures, only to have the device freeze on him at the precise moment he needed it most.

"The program isn't starting!" he shouted frantically.

"You've got to be kidding!"

"It isn't working!"

"Check the parameters. The door has to be there. Hit the data switch!"

"I can't find it!"

"Maybe I can locate it manually," Dan shouted. "I made it easy to find for just such occasions. Stay here so I can find my way back to center." He started out towards the left, pacing quickly and counting his steps. Just ten steps away, it happened quietly.

A rock from a nearby building tumbled from high above and landed next to Daniel Blank. It exploded in a cloud of dust, a cloud through which Max and Sarah could barely see as Dan knelt down to collect himself after the near miss. With his head down, he didn't see as the rest of that building slowly lean, about to follow. Max and Sarah saw all too well. They could not speak for the fear. But, they watched as Dan Blank knelt on one knee, looking towards the ground, as an entire building collapsed around him.

"DAD!" Max shouted as he rushed towards his father.

"Max, think about this. You can't help him that way! We have to get home. Then, we can return and save him, but we have to get home first!" Sarah shouted.

Furiously, Max turned to that tablet and started hitting button after button. Whatever had been frozen previously had somehow been fixed.

After 30 seconds of working, Max announced, "Got it!"

He took Sarah by the hand and started the five steps towards the door that had just appeared. He was halfway through the doorway when he felt a sudden absence of Sarah's hand. It was, for a brief moment, like he was holding onto a ghost. He could feel a shadow of her warmth, could almost still touch her. He turned back, just as he went through the door, just in time to see the love of his life crushed by a falling wall of rock. Everything went white before Max's eyes. He couldn't think. He couldn't breathe. He was pretty sure he didn't want to live anymore.

Chapter 19

Both women wore pained expressions at the end of the story. It was almost as if they could smell the dust as it rose and could vividly see the fear in Max and Sarah's faces right before calamity struck. Worst of all, they could feel the depth and all-encompassing magnitude of Max's grief.

"And that was it," Max said. "In a future city that I'd never seen before, somewhere Dad had visited at some point on his solo travels. They died as time crumbled and contracted around them."

"I'm so sorry Max," Rachel said.

"I'd always envisioned you all taking Sarah into the system against her will," Becca said, "but she loved the work, huh?"

"Yes, she did. Almost as much as I loved her." Max replied somberly. He never felt like he could adequately express his loss. Words didn't come close.

Becca looked at him for a long time with some degree of forgiveness passing over her face, "I'm still pissed that you all weren't more careful. But, I can see now that I've placed all the blame on you over the years wrongly. You deserved some of it. Not all of it."

"Max," Rachel started, "I'm sure there is an answer to this, but why haven't you gone back to save them? After all, you have a time machine."

Max nodded at the obviousness of the question, "I've tried. I spent five years of my life trying. But, some things can't be unwritten."

"You mean once something happens," Becca clarified, "It can't be changed?"

"The system only grants so much power to override on things like life and death. Or, more specifically, the laws of physics and biology tend to remain inflexible. You can't undo death, even with a time machine."

"So, you tried everything?"

"I did. Everything and more," Max said with surety. "And, I almost lost myself in the process. When your life revolves around going to visit, and try to save, the dead...you aren't really alive yourself. I spent years visiting with ghosts, reliving moments. I have not loved since that day. But, I almost stopped living too."

"Max, I saw you with those girls at the pool. The way they spoke to you, I know that you all have—"

"That," Max interrupted Rachel, "is different. It's complex. It fills a void, but leaves one too."

Becca cringed at the reference to Max's love life. She might have partially forgiven him. It was still a lot to stomach to listen to the husband of your dead sister refer to his later exploits. Rachel pressed on, slightly insensitive to the ways in which this conversation was affecting Becca.

"Is this another one of those times where you aren't telling us everything, Max?" Rachel asked.

"I can't...not yet anyways."

"What is it Max?" She asked.

"There's a reason that I don't want to go back," he said. Both girls looked at him with a mixture of dread and interest. What he had to say was obviously serious; did they really want to hear it?

Both Becca Baxter and Rachel Austin sat quietly for a long while, as if they were contemplating just how deeply they wanted to dig into this man's obviously fragile and tortured psyche. They looked to each other, both silently asking the other to ask the question, neither willing. Becca had too many other things running through her mind right now to press on for more. If she'd had her druthers, they all would have sat quietly for a few months. Each of these women had their own unique conceptions of Max, and despite her fatigue, they both did want him to explain things. Rachel's curiosity and, to some degree, professional responsibility—she was with him to do a job, after all—finally stirred a question.

"Why don't you want to tell us this, Max?"

"Because someone might figure something out. Something that I have tried to keep hidden for a very long time."

"What's that?" Becca asked before visibly having a thought. "Figure something out? Did it have to do with the riddle Sarah told me about this company?

"She told you the riddle..."

"Yes, she wrote it at the end of several letters to me. I'm fascinated by riddles. I've always liked them. She knew that. I used go through the weekend papers and parse out the solutions crossword puzzles. This one, though, I never got."

"What's the riddle?" Rachel asked.

Becca started, "When everything is natural, no one notices. When something is unnatural, everyone notices. Nature is the only place—"

Max began to speak over her and she stopped, "Where nothing can be natural or unnatural because everything must coexist. There is power in paradox and it is the way to find what is natural and what is unnatural."

"What?"

"My thoughts exactly." Max answered with resignation, "My father frequently told me that riddle from the time I was young. He said it could save my life in here."

"In here," Rachel said to herself and the others. "Why in here, Max?"

"Huh?"

She looked at him with a perplexed expression, "The wording suggests we are in a certain place, not in a certain time."

"It is just an expression. By 'in here,' I always thought he meant that it was in the time system itself or maybe just the pods."

"So this is your father's expression?"

"Yes, he always used that riddle, in here," Max seemed to be scrambling a bit as he answered.

Ever the investigator, Rachel pressed forward, "You didn't want us to know the riddle, or is there more to this baggage that you have been carrying for so long?"

"Let's go," Max ignored her question and pulled his computer out of a bag on his side. "I'll create a doorway here that will take us back to our time. I will get you two out and then come back for the others."

Neither woman moved for a few seconds, then Rachel asked, "So, everything was a diversion for them? They aren't even in real danger?"

"That's right," Max said. "I had to separate Becca. I couldn't face her parents again to tell them about another daughter that was lost in time. If something had happened while she was with Dale Brooks, I would not have been able to undo it. Now, come on!"

Becca looked at Max for a second or two and a wave of empathy and gratitude washed over her, "I do thank you for coming in here to get me, Max. When I saw we were at Time Vacation I feared that I was dead. I can't even stomach those commercials anymore. They give me nightmares."

"That is a reasonable fear. In many ways, I share it," Max said as he worked on that tablet, pressing buttons. "This will just take a moment."

As he said those words, he immediately doubted them. He was struck by an almost visceral fear. The story he'd just told still rang in his ears, and it sounded a whole lot like the sounds now happening outside the windows. His fearful shaking and panic began as the two women turned towards the windows to learn what Max knew.

"Max," Rachel said, "something weird is going on out there."

"What is that?" Max tried to stall as he kept plugging away at the controls, even though he knew exactly what they were referencing. He knew it all too well.

"The buildings outside are falling."

"Is this…" Becca trailed off.

Her question was answered as Max grew angrier at his tablet and shouted at it, "Come on! Not again you damn machine."

"What's happening?" Rachel shouted, though she didn't know if she wanted to hear the answer.

"Time is collapsing."

"Well, get us out of here."

"I'm working as fast as I can, Rachel."

"Maybe work a bit faster, huh, Max?" Becca said, trying to express both urgency and calm. As she said it, though, all feelings of calm dissolved. They were replaced with a pit in her stomach. A stomach that then leapt up in her chest as the floor beneath her trembled once, trembled again, and then collapsed.

"Max!" both women shouted simultaneously as the hotel began to crumble with them inside it.

"Grab onto me!" he replied, "Almost got it!"

Overhead, the ceiling was coming down upon them as the floor began to fall out from beneath them, resulting in a deafening

150

weightlessness. Both Rachel and Becca reached their hands out towards Max to grab onto his jacket. As they did, the wind gusted and light flashed. They were saved. But, where were they?

Chapter 20

Dale Brooks and Ron Hess had yet to come to physical blows, but it wasn't for a lack of tension. Mostly, the reasons for their lack of violence were due to a mutual need. In a strange land and foreign time, it felt like there was some strength in numbers, even if some in that number weren't *total* allies. But, the lack of overt fighting was also born out of a mutual fascination with each other's story.

"How the hell did you find us here?" Dale asked before clarifying, "Actually, I'm interested in how the hell we got here. But, also in how you showed up in the same damn war zone."

"I don't know that the word 'we' applies. All we did was bring in Max. He found you here, or put you here. Then, he left us. " Ron shrugged his shoulders.

"Maximilian Blank? I never thought in a million years that he would help you or anyone at Time Vacation."

"I think you properly estimated his hatred of me. But, you underestimated his feelings of obligations towards Becca Baxter. If you'd left her alone instead of kidnapping her, he would never have helped. He came on board to protect her, not to help us."

"We didn't kidnap her," Dale said, though his tone suggested that he knew this protestation was a bit weak and quite possibly false, "We are paying her. She agreed to come."

"You know as well as I do that lying to someone about what they are getting into mitigates any agreement they make. You misrepresented who you were and what you were planning to do."

"Whatever we did, I still don't understand what Max' allegiance to her is based on. And, why the hell is she so afraid of being in the past?" Brad Hammer asked. "I'd have thought that someone as interested in history as she is would have been excited to come along."

"You don't know?" Eco said in disbelief.

"Apparently not, because I don't know what you are referencing. Know what?" Brad asked.

"Yeah," Dale agreed. "I don't know what you're talking about. And, I certainly don't understand why Max feels such an obligation to Becca. I was not even aware that he knew her."

"Becca's sister was Sarah."

"Sarah?" Brad asked thickly.

"Sarah Blank. She died in the accident with Dan Blank during the experimentation stage. She was Max's wife."

"Shit," Dale said. "That explains a whole hell of a lot."

"Yeah, I feel bad now. What did we put her through, bringing her into the system that killed her sister," Brad's voice was thick with sympathy and regret.

Eco chided them, "Try to show her some respect and empathy, maybe not act like hard-ass dudes who don't have a clue."

Dale and Brad both nodded, signaling that they would if they ever saw her again. They hoped to see Becca again, but mainly because if they did see her chances were she'd be with Max. He was pretty much their only hope right now.

"What about the other woman one of you mentioned? The one with Max now?"

"That's Rachel Austin. She is some sort of special agent with the FBI. She was sent in to make sure you guys were either pulled out or killed in the system," Ron answered.

"Well, that is partially good news. Because she'll have a hard time doing that if they never find us," Dale said as he simultaneously reached an awareness of just how screwed he was. If she found him, he'd be arrested. If she didn't, he'd never make it out of this place.

Quest, who'd been sitting quietly and gazing out the window into the streets below, spoke up, "I want to know how you guys intend to get away with what you are doing?" He paused, "The FBI has Time Vacation surrounded. The only reason they are not going in is that they don't want a shootout. There is no leaving the building. Even if you find your fabled treasure, what good is a bunch of gold if you spend the next 30 years of your life in jail?"

"Ah, that's where you are wrong," Dale said proudly. "Once we have the location of the ships, we are going to go to a point in time when Dennis has the journals and has contacted me. We are going to slip a map into the journal so that we can find the ships nice and easy."

"The idea being that you then won't even need to go back?"

"In the future."

"You mean the past?"

"Whatever. The point being, we will tell ourselves how to find the ships without going back in time again. If we have the maps and info, we won't have had to go back into the past, in the future, again. We will have avoided this whole thing."

Ron was shaking his head emphatically. He knew that what they were suggesting would not work, "That would be a massive time paradox."

"Huh?" Brad mumbled dumbly.

"It won't work. Because to get the map you have to go back, therefore you cannot have the map without going back. Your plan, it won't work."

Despite all of the stupid mistakes he'd made over the previous months, and his record of ignorance, Dale had enough disdain for Ron to disregard any knowledge he might have over this system he'd successfully run as a business for years. His hubris was remarkable.

"No, we simply change the timeline to an alternate one. It's very simple. I'll just reconfigure..."

"Dale, when will you learn? Nothing about time travel is simple."

Eco interrupted, her voice sharp, "That's not the..."

"Enough discussion," Ron said. "I'm not interested in trying to convince him right now. We have practical matters of survival to attend to here and now. We need to figure out what we do next. I say we need to be proactive about finding Max, Rachel, and Becca. Then, we can go home."

"Not without the map we don't!" Dale said.

"To hell with you and your damn map, Dale. Anyway, you don't have a ton of leverage in this scenario."

"I'm not leaving without them," Dale replied. "And I know that you all have been ordered to bring me back."

"You will come with us or you'll die…"

WHOOSH

As Dale spoke, a rush of wind entered the bank building. Papers flew off the desks, one cup of pens hit the floor and scattered noisily on marble.

"Another time jump," Eco announced to the group, "Brace yourselves." Her words echoed throughout that bank lobby as a tremendous white light burst through the air. When it faded, the bank was empty of people.

Chapter 21

When they landed, Becca lay on her side. She immediately started dusting herself off. Max was once again on top of Rachel. Repeating their old joke, Rachel put her hands on his shoulders and pushed him playfully away.

"Now still isn't the right time."

"Agreed," Max replied, "though that's twice now that I've saved your life."

"Saved my life? You are the one who was punching wrong button after wrong button. A little shaky there with the entire universe crumbling around, huh?" Rachel ribbed Max. She was indeed grateful for his quick thinking and heroic actions. She'd have to figure out a way to demonstrate her gratitude later. She had a few things in mind.

Though the women didn't know where they were after narrowly escaping the collapse of time, Max knew it all too well. It was a fancy room, with plush pillows of deep red and gold piping. It had a leather couch in one corner with deep leather chairs opposite the couch. The room had lower ceilings than one would expect, though. When Rachel looked over towards the light streaming through small circular windows, she understood why.

"Are we on a ship?"

"Yes," Max answered.

"Some ship!" said Becca. "It's nicer than most any hotel I've ever been to. Look at this table set for two. That's real silver, and that looks hand painted! Must have cost a fortune; those German masters never work for cheap! I remember looking for wedding china with Sarah. She loved this kind of thing."

"The décor could just be classic, but I think we are in the past somewhere. Max, am I right?" Rachel said as she picked up a cocktail shrimp off the hand painted plate in front of her. "Good food!"

Max didn't answer. When she saw the pained look on his face, she toned down a bit on the glib commentary. Becca had already noticed his expression and clammed up herself. They both waited for Max to speak.

"I don't know why it brought us here. Of all the places to bring us, it brought us here. Son of a bitch machine…"

"Where are we, Max?"

"This is where Sarah and I would go for our anniversary. A very special place where we would spend a few days. You are right, Becca. She loved the silver, the china, the little touches of luxury."

"Okay, so you and Sarah came here. But, that still doesn't explain where 'here' is. Where are we?"

"Oh, I suspect you'll discover that soon enough," he paused, "and when you do, you'll wish you hadn't."

Becca was confused. Max knew where they were, but it wasn't where he'd wanted them to end up. This stuff was all so confusing.

"So," she asked, "what do we do?"

"I didn't have time to open a door. So, I ordered a jump." Max answered.

"You can order jumps?"

"That's what I was doing so rapidly on my computer."

"Well, if you can order jumps, order us one now and jump us back to our time. I'm ready for a long hot bath in my own city and year! For all I care, you can leave Dale Brooks and that group wherever they are."

"I ordered a jump then because I have no other choice, but we may be here for a while."

"Why?"

"I wish I could explain it more thoroughly, but much of this is still a mystery to me. The human mind is a fussy thing. If you exit the system in a way that you didn't enter, the mind does not accept it. We aren't sure why. We are sure, though, of the consequences."

"What happens?" Becca asked.

"You go crazy. The longest anyone has lasted after being pulled out through a different portal was about five hours."

"They went crazy after that?"

"No. They went crazy right away. The instant the exited the pod they were biting themselves, ripping at their own skin, and trying to slam their head into any hard surface they could find."

"What happened after that?"

"People kill themselves. They throw themselves off heights. They use knives. Swallow boiling water. Crazy stuff."

"Is there any way we can go back the way we came, since that world just collapsed all around us? Or are we just locked here for an indeterminate amount of time?"

"Yes, we can get back to our own time," Max answered, sounding confident now. "I just have to get that doorway open. And, we have to go through with everyone we came with. The good news is, everyone else should be here now. I pulled them into the jump with us."

"Everyone, meaning Eco, Zone, Ron?"

"Yeah, and Dale's crew too. However much you might want them to remain trapped Becca, we had to bring them with us," Max answered. "Follow me and pay attention—you may have to get back to this room soon."

As they walked out of the room and down one hallway, both girls looked at the brass lights accompanying every door and the floral carpeting on the floors. There was a picture of a red flag, about the size of a photograph, with a single white star on each door under the numbers.

"I have a feeling that I've seen this place before." Becca announced, "But in pictures, not in real life."

"That would not surprise me," answered Max. "Pretty much everyone who has been to the movies has seen this place."

As they came around the next corner, they could hear loud arguing coming through a door to the left.

"That sounds like Ron," Max said. "Good, we found them."

The room was filled with familiar faces, but no one looked up as they entered. They were all circled around a figure laying on the floor. When Becca leaned over, she could see who it was. It was the one member of their expedition who'd regularly treated her with respect. The one guy that had been somewhat kind. He didn't look good.

"Baljeet," she said quietly.

"He didn't make it," Ron announced. "He's dead."

Chapter 22

The room was quiet for a long time. Ron Hess looked quietly at his former employee turned traitor. Ron knew, deep down, that he had driven Baljeet to some of his actions. And, he knew now better than ever before that many of the clever techie's criticisms of Time Vacation had been on the money. He had seen early on that it was a place built upon greed. Now, he was dead. Ron had enough bitterness to feel that it was slightly justified, but he also had enough humanity to dread what he knew he'd have to do: tell Baljeet's family. He had a loving wife and kids.

Some of the travelers hadn't known him as well, but Dale Brooks and his associates felt even more nervous than they'd felt over the last hours. Their only true ally in all this with any real understanding of the system in which they were trapped was now dead. Moreover, what had happened to him was mysterious and seemingly arbitrary. Why hadn't they died too? Now, Dale, Brad, and Dennis were entirely and completely at the mercy of Max and Ron. And, just as bitterly, their search for massive treasure was now surely hopeless. They'd have to face the authorities. There would be no explaining. Jail time was not just a possibility, it was a certainty.

"How did it happen?" Rachel asked.

"Couldn't survive this many time jumps," Max replied, though Rachel read into that tone the same element of intentional ambiguity. She didn't know if the others caught it, but she didn't think that Max really believed that explanation. What had happened then?

"I've never heard of someone dying after so few," Eco said in confusion. "We've done more jumps than this in our old roles."

Zone replied defensively, "Not jumps like this. Not this complex and stressful."

Max looked briefly at Zone with slightly squinted eyes but didn't say much. Then, Eco turned to their leader.

"What are we supposed to do now?"

The question brought Max back to the matter at hand, "We just need to wait it out for a moment. There will be a door that appears on this ship to take us home."

"When?"

"I don't know, Dale. It's triggered by an event."

"What event?"

"Damn all your questions, Brooks. I'm not your tour guide or personal search engine." Max snapped before continuing angrily, "Follow me."

The group walked behind him. Becca was first in line, then Ron and his employees. Behind them came Dale, Brad Hammer, and Dennis Fast. Rachel trailed that trio to make sure none of them got any crazy ideas about escaping. Where they'd escape to, she didn't know. But, she knew well what they were facing upon return. She'd seen enough criminals flee to know that fear could motivate unwise choices. As she closed the door and followed the others into the hallway, she looked one last time at the body of Baljeet. Whoever found him would be shocked, not just by the corpse, but by its nationality. Given the estimated time period, he was probably the only Indian on board. She locked the door as she shut it behind her.

They traipsed down the hallway, passing some other passengers along the way who really paid them no heed. It was late at night and many of the passengers seemed just a bit tipsy. Max led them out to a deck towards the bow of the ship. Behind them, four large steam stacks puffed out a dark smoke. The wind was bitter cold. Above them, they could see stars. They were vivid and brilliant against the dark sky, not so much visible as screaming of the mystery of the universe. They were stunning.

"Set up here for just a bit," Max said to the group, "We need to wait on the signal."

Most of the travelers went to the railing, peered down at the cold water being sliced by the ship's speed. Rachel walked over towards Max, they stood away from the rest of the group, and she put her hand on his shoulder. She wondered at the last minute if she should play her hand so aggressively.

"Max, I want to ask you something. I think I may have figured out what it is you are hiding."

"What do you mean, Rachel?"

"You'd mentioned earlier that it was always nice to have more knowledge than the rest of us. Well, I think I may have been thinking about that too simply. I was thinking of some of the smaller incidents. It helped when I started thinking about it on a bigger scale. I can't stop contemplating those women at the pool. The way they looked at you, and the way that I look at you."

"Let's talk about this later, huh?" Max nodded and glanced in the opposite direction. Rachel turned to see that, less than dodging her inquisitions, Max's answer probably had something to do with the crewmember heading straight towards them. A younger gentleman, short and fit, approached. He looked official in his white slacks and jacket, official and proud of it. A blue hat rested just above his ears. He approached them with a purpose. Rachel read the insignia and wording on his hat and chest pocket, "White Star Line."

White Star Line, she thought. *How do I know that name?*

"Excuse me, sir, ma'am," the young employee spoke, "I am sure you all remember, but we've asked that passengers not come out on this deck. It's cold outside and the seas are a bit rough tonight. It's for your own safety..." he trailed off as voice rang out in the crow's nest high above.

"Iceberg! Straight ahead! Iceberg!"

The crewmember almost crouched at that announcement. He turned to Rachel and Max quickly, "Inside. Now." The young man dashed away, his obligations shifted.

Max called to the others, "That would be our signal! We don't have much time. Run!"

Everyone dashed after him. Behind him, he heard Eco huff, "The White Star Line? Icebergs? This is the damn Titanic."

They went back through the same door that they'd come out of, but they took a right this time instead of heading all the way back to where they'd come from. This hallway led them out into a grand lobby, replete with a massive curved staircase and crystal chandeliers. They ran up the staircase, noticing as they did the string quartet playing one of Bach's suites. They ran through an upper lobby area, and had just come through a swinging set of double doors when: *Boom! Crkckck.*

The sound of impact was remarkable. It was as if the ship was a tin can and some massive Titan of old had crunched it in his hand. The floor on which they were standing shuddered. Everyone was thrown off balance and collapsed with a distinct lack of grace. Max picked himself up first.

"Come on. That means we have about 30 seconds."

They all scrambled up and hurried after their leader, entirely dependent on his word and wisdom. They dashed around one corner, then another. Finally, they came to an open doorway. Beside it, a sign read, "Library, Reading Room."

Through the doorway, in front of a rich wooden shelves and massive books of deep reds, blues, and greens, glowed the portal they were looking for. Max didn't slow as he came through the door, and sprinted towards that glowing window into where it was he wanted to return. Just as he reached the time door, though, it snapped shut with a whoosh and he crashed into the bookshelves. Those following most closely behind him, Becca and Ron, fell on top of him. The others were able to stop in time.

"Shit!" Max said from under the pile of Shakespeare plays and two people, "That was our one way out!"

"How the hell did we get here anyways?" Ron asked.

"Sarah and I used to vacation here."

"On this ship or this route?" Eco prodded further.

"Both. We'd get on in South Hampton and ride until it hit the berg. We would use that door to escape."

"How did that door appear for us this time?"

Max responded with the lack of detail or specifics that they'd all come to dread and expect, "It's a long story."

"Sure it is," Ron groaned. "I'd love an answer with some specifics when you get the time though."

"How do we get out now?" Zone asked.

"I don't know," Max admitted reluctantly.

"We can wait for another door, right?" Eco volunteered, "After a jump, a door always comes."

"Not this time. Not with as many jumps as we've taken."

"There must be some sort of option," Quest prodded.

"I need to think. No one leave this room. Better yet, leave this room and take your fate into your own feeble hands. Otherwise, wait here. Rachel, come with me."

Chapter 23

Rachel walked dutifully behind Max as they left the reading room and entered the hallway. The rest of the group sat bitter and quiet. It was infuriating to be caught in a reality they didn't understand, and even more frustrating to rely upon someone so hell-bent on keeping secrets. Max led Rachel down a hallway, past a couple turns, before he turned down the third corridor and they were once more on the deck of the ship. Max walked over to a bench that looked out on the moving ocean.

"Sit."

Up above these two visitors from another time, in the pilothouse of the ship, the first mate was giving his report to the Captain of this ill-fated ship.

"Mr. Murdock, what was that?

"Iceberg, sir. The watch saw it, but we weren't far out when he did. Probably quarter mile at the most. I pulled us hard to starboard and then tried to port 'round her, but she hit."

"Close all the gates."

"I already did, sir," the first mate nodded.

"Good. I want a full inspection and a report immediately."

"Of course, sir."

They hadn't been able to feel it when they were inside the ship, but once you were outside and looking down at the water, you could see that the ship was starting to lean sharply in one direction. They could also, when the leaned over the port side of the boat, see what seemed to be the upper part of a tremendous gash in the ship's hull.

"Geez. That is a serious hole. How much time before the ship sinks?" Rachel asked Max, her voice somehow calm.

"About two hours," he answered quickly enough to suggest that he'd been thinking the same thing himself.

"North Atlantic. April 14th, 1912," Rachel said almost to herself.

Max's ears perked up, "You know your history."

"I've always loved the story of the Titanic. I think it is really romantic that you and Sarah rode it."

Max stared out onto the ocean and sighed deeply with regret and sadness, "It was her favorite spot."

"Max," Rachel once again placed her hands on his left elbow, "I want to ask you what I started to ask you about earlier."

"Go ahead. That is what I wanted to discuss with you, too."

Rachel didn't really know how to ask the question. If she was wrong, she was going to sound totally crazy. But, she was pretty sure she wasn't wrong, "This is not real, right?" She blurted out.

"What do you mean by *this*?"

"Well, let me start with those girls at the pool."

"What about them? Beauties, right…"

"That is putting it mildly. And that is part of my point. I've seen women that beautiful. When you live in New York, you see

172

your fare share of models. What I have not ever seen is women that look like that who looked at men the way those girls looked at you."

"What are you getting at, Rachel?"

"I've tried to figure out this system for years. And, I am not a dumb woman. But, there were always so many things I just couldn't get. And, the way those women looked at you reminded me of something in a video game or something. It wasn't real. It was total desire, but it was what you wanted from them. They couldn't have flipped that switch so quickly. And, no woman I've ever seen would broadcast an openness to anyone like that—not even Max Blank."

"I think I'm pretty great!" Max joked.

"So do I," Rachel said. "I'm more attracted to you than I've been to any man in a long time. But, I'd never look at you *that* way. I'd be losing any influence I could possibly hope to have in the future. But, that isn't even all. They both looked at you like that. Both of them. And, they didn't seem to have any jealousy between them."

"Jealousy?" Max asked.

"No women can share a man like that. They can be open to adventurous things. But, when they look at you with absolute desire, and are perfectly happy to share, those things don't jive together."

Max laughed, "Impressive detective!"

She paused for a bit as she thought about how to phrase this next part, "This isn't real. We've never traveled through time. Am I right?"

"You are."

"Time travel isn't possible, is it Max?"

"I wouldn't go that far. In fact, I think it probably is possible. But time travel was not what my father discovered."

"So," Rachel motioned towards the ship's railing, the bubbling ocean water below, "What is all of this?"

"What do you think it is Rachel?"

"Some sort of insanely lucid group dream, maybe?"

"Not exactly. It is a Virtual Reality system. VR for short."

"What?"

"Everything at Time Vacation is for show. It's a complicated virtual reality system. Like a complicated video game where you can no longer see the real world, and so the virtual temporarily becomes reality."

"So, those women…you created them for yourself?"

"They are one of the most consistently enjoyable parts of this system for me, yeah."

Rachel thought for a second, "It certainly feels real. I mean, this ship is like something from the movies. It is amazing, actually. But, why the whole Time Vacation shtick? Why call it time travel?"

"Well, Rachel, my dad's brilliance wasn't of the technical so much as business variety. He figured out how to get the human mind to respond to a computer, or to sink absolutely into a computer. Think about it for a minute. If the common person knew that they could use a standard computer and about five hundred dollars' worth of parts from Radio Shack to create anything they ever wanted, what would happen?"

"They would do it," she answered. "Everyone would do it."

"Think further down the line," Max prodded. "What then?"

"Ah..." It dawned on her, "It would be the end of everything."

"Society as we know it would crash and burn. Who's going to go to work when instead, they can sleep with any person of their choosing, in exactly the level of detail and style of their design?"

"I wouldn't," Rachel replied honestly.

"Who would go sell insurance, or pick up garbage, when instead they could spend their days as Frodo fighting to destroy a terribly evil ring, or Harry Potter working to defeat Voldemort, or Marty McFly on his hover board?"

"Not many, I'm guessing."

"How many women would show up at their nursing job, or go to class to learn how to be a doctor, when instead they could dream away into the body of Angelina Jolie as Laura Croft, or dance in front of thousands as Madonna?"

"I'd prefer a day as Laura Croft to a day at the office," Rachel laughed, "though I'm more of an Aniston girl than Jolie."

"So many women are!"

"But, you still haven't answered the time travel bit. Why not just call this system what it is rather than lying about time travel."

"Well, we knew we needed to keep the technology secret, somehow. So, time travel did two things. It acted as a nice cover, one that was so complicated people would assume it futile to try to break through. In the meantime, it could make us really rich."

"You could make more money this way?"

"We thought so. After all, what better way to get people to spend millions of dollars than to promise them a unique experience? The notion that they were *really* traveling back in time made it even more special. And, special equals dollars. Lots and lots of dollars. By saying it was time travel, dad could charge a million dollars a trip, and people would pay it."

"So, what is creating this world for us right now?"

"We have super computers that run the system. When you step into your pod, they create a unique experience for each person. It is quite elegant actually. Elegant and massive. They are the largest hard drives in the world. And, you can set the controls so that everyone's VR integrates with everyone else's. In other words, my computer is working with yours."

"How does the system have this level of detail?"

"The computerization of everything has really helped. We sample an online version of history book, or pictures, even modern movies. We put them into the computer, which integrates that particular information with a massive database of similar worlds. Algorithm's do the rest. Just like Google can see that you are searching for a new purse and sends you ads for luggage and hand baggage companies, when we give our machine some starting information, it can predict the rest. It fills in the structure."

"I think I get it," Rachel answered.

"For example," Max said, "The war city to which I took those others was a test we had designed. It incorporates a number of different wars and cities, and the main road just loops around seamlessly. They thought they were walking in circles, but they were really just wandering around the entirety of that particular segment of VR."

"What are the limits of this thing?" Rachel asked.

"Not many," answered Max proudly. "After this many years, the system has enough data in it to create any place and any time you could possibly want. And, if you did find something missing, programing new realities is intuitive and easy."

"Okay, if this is all a fake reality, then what really happened to your wife and father?"

"The story I told was true. They died investigating jumps. Not time jumps, but all computers have slight problems with their systems. Jumps occur. We wanted to see if we could pinpoint the reason. They were trying to move from reality to reality without coming out first."

"So, if my body is back in my pod at your cabin, and is perfectly safe, how could I die here? How did they die?"

"Well, they were so entrenched in the realities...the fear they felt was real. When you die in a virtual reality, that is enough to kill the body in the pod."

"I don't understand why," Rachel said.

"When the mind experiences death, there's no saving the body. You die in here and you are dead. And what I said was also true about coming out. The belief is so powerful in the mind, that even if you know this is virtual reality, you must be brought out the right way or you will not be able to handle it."

"So, Baljeet?"

"Baljeet experienced death in his own vision of this story. I'm not sure what that experience was yet that caused it. But, he died here and his body is dead in the pod. There was nothing I could do for him once we arrived."

"The women at the hotel?" Rachel asked.

"Yeah, I created them. The hotel was my own personal vacation. I could never love another woman after what had happened, but a man has needs. I used the system for my own personal pleasure."

"I also noticed that many of the characters we saw, the waitress at the bar, the bellhop at the hotel, they reminded me of other people."

Max nodded, "I plugged in a couple specific celebrities, and the system merged them together for me to create a unique experience."

"Even that would get old eventually though, right?"

"Not really," Max answered. "It can be as unpredictable as real life, but you can put certain parameters in place. And, you can program for tons of experiences. You didn't meet all of the women at that hotel, but you would have seen many of them look at me the same way."

"Well, what happens to them when the hotel collapsed?"

"The program shut down. Think of it like your computer freezing up. Since they are a part of the program, when you restart it, everything is back to the way it was."

"But we have no restarts? Our bodies just die?" Rachel asked.

"That's right."

"Is there another way out?"

"There is one thing that might work. I've never had it work, but it is the only choice we have."

Just then, the ship listed a bit more to its side. The crew was frantic above them trying to ready the lifeboats. With the sudden increase in the lean of the ship, the passengers that had previously been fairly well behaved grew much more animated in their demands that the crew hurry.

"What is that one?"

"It's the paradox."

"What about it?"

"We disrupt the system enough. Change enough things, and the system will realize that something has gone wrong. It will give us a door that will take us back to reality.

"But that's dangerous? I can hear it in your voice."

Max looked out at the ocean. The first lifeboats were slowly lowering into the water. From there, passengers would climb down rope ladders to get into their salvation. They'd have to hope that they could get far enough away before the ship sank, suctioning down with it anyone or thing that was too close. This death would not have been his first choice, to put it mildly. In fact, drowning was usually the most vivid of his nightmares.

"That's the paradox of it. The system may become unstable and shut the whole works down before the door comes."

"And then we're dead too?"

"As surely as if we were to plunge into that ice cold water," Max agreed as he motioned out towards the ocean.

"You have no other ways?"

"No. With my computer here I can jump around within the system. I can make anything I want to happen." Max paused, "I can't make a door out, though. Here, I'll show you. Look up."

Rachel turned her head skyward as Max pressed some buttons and swiped a few things on his computer. It started with one star that moved. It shifted slightly in the sky. Then, there were five more moving. They seemed to all move in concert, making some shape. Suddenly, Rachel made it out: it was a massive heart. Then, almost like an artist adding emphasis, Max made some emphatic gestures with his fingertips. Suddenly, from across the sky, a group of stars merged together and formed an arrow, an arrow that flew across the sky and lodged right in the middle of the heart."

Rachel was not the sentimental sort. She'd never demanded flowers or chocolates on Valentine's Day. Hallmark cards weren't her thing either. The combination of sadness and brilliance in this man standing opposite her, and this gesture, melted her heart. She should have been furious with him for misleading her along with the others. She should have been bitter about the years she'd wasted investigating time travel. She ought to have hated him. As someone involved in the legal world, she should have been thinking about all the ramifications of this fraud he'd perpetuated against so many unassuming clients. But, she'd never felt more attracted to anyone in her life at that precise moment.

Max explained, "I can make you a heart here. But, I can't make a door to get out."

Rachel thought to herself, fleetingly, that a door to get out was the wrong idea entirely. Why leave? Then, she looked around her at the people fearfully preparing to board lifeboats. She thought of Sarah Blank. And, she wanted very much to get back home safely.

"Why not?"

"There are limitations to the system's code in order to keep it stable."

"Then what are we going to do?"

"You are in this with me now. I say we vote on it." Max waited a second before continuing, "The entire group must be in on this." He started towards the door to get the others.

"Max, wait a minute, will you please?"

"What?"

"This is just so...amazing. I like portions of this virtual reality more than the real world. Can you hold me here for a bit?"

"Hold you?"

"Yeah, I want to look up at the stars from your arms? I want to admire your handiwork."

"I guess we have time for that," Max conceded happily.

They looked upwards. The heart had dissolved, and the sky was a sea of yellows and whites and blues. Some of the stars flickered more than others. One streaked across the sky, and Rachel made her wish silently.

"This may be all we ever have, Max."

"I feel like, after so many years of searching, I just found you. The chances of us getting out of this thing alive are slim."

"Then hold me for a few more minutes," Rachel said. She reached up and put her hands on his arms, pulling his embrace even tighter, clinging to him as he stood behind her.

"You don't care about those other women you saw?"

"How many women were there?"

"Lots," Max admitted.

"Well, I can't imagine what you've been through, losing a wife. I am sure you did what you needed to survive the grief. But, the thing that makes me feel lots better about it all," she looked back at him and grinned, "is that they weren't real. It might have felt like reality, but it wasn't. I can give you reality. And, it'll be better than anything you ever thought to program! I've got tricks you've never seen."

"I've felt something for you ever since I first saw you at the cabin," Max said, unsure of where to take the conversation after that aggressive and attractive offer.

"Me too," Rachel said and continued, "but when we get back, Max. Is one woman gonna be enough for you?"

"Depends on the woman," he said as he spun this particular woman around to kiss her deeply and passionately. She'd been waiting for the moment across hundreds of years now. Too often anticipation of such magnitude leads to experiences that can't match up. Such was not the case with this kiss. With this kiss, everything she'd imagined was there. Everything and more.

Chapter 24

For his part, Max felt something different kissing Rachel. As amazing and awesome as those virtual scenarios had been, knowing that there was an autonomous human being kissing back just felt different. He leaned back, caught his breath, and kissed her again. Yep. This was different. Another roll and rumble of the ship reminded them that there was little time to indulge in their newly blossoming romance.

"Let's go get the others," Max said.

They made their way back, walking against the steady stream of passengers now fleeing to the ship's decks frantically, and even more frantically arguing about who would get seats in the lifeboats. When they made it back to the reading room, Max was relieved to find the others had followed his orders and stayed put. To try to find them again, on this massive ship, would have been impossible.

"Thank God you're back!" Eco said. "You know, a bit of an explanation would be helpful and much appreciated."

"You aren't gonna get the full story right now. But, here's the deal in brief," Max said, "I cannot get us back to our time from this one. The only chance we have is to destroy the whole system. None of you really understand what a big deal that is, but it is risky to say the least."

Rachel glanced at him knowingly, noticing that his choice of words was now vague enough to apply to virtual reality or time travel. Maybe he was honoring what he'd told her just then.

"But, in trying to destroy the whole system...confuse it really, there is also the chance that we could all die."

Ron spoke first, "There's also a chance we get out, right?"

"Yes, there is a chance we get out."

"And it is the only chance we have of getting out," Brad Hammer asked nervously.

"That's true too."

"Then obviously we go for it, right?" volunteered Dale.

"I agree," said Zone.

"Is there anyone here that does not agree?"

"What would we say instead," Zone quipped, "that we'd prefer to stay on the Titanic?"

"What can we do to make this as safe as possible?" Quest asked.

"Very little," Max said. "But follow my directions impeccably and we give ourselves the best shot."

The mood around the room was not positive. They'd been following Max's directions for a while now and still didn't know what the hell was going on. On the other hand, they really didn't have a choice. He'd gotten them through this much, and didn't seem to have a vendetta. He really was their only hope.

"No objections?" Max asked. No one spoke up.

He pulled out his computer and hit a few buttons first. Once the machine was up and humming, his pace increased dramatically. As he typed, he started to speak to the group.

"Now, when Sarah and I were coming here we anticipated problems. So, we had a spot filled with supplies."

At this, Max stopped and walked over to the bookshelves. He climbed up the ladder to the very top, reached towards a plain looking book. Instead of pulling it off the shelf, though, he reached up further and towards the top of spine. There, he pressed a small button that was hidden from down below. Suddenly, part of the case below him swiveled out to reveal an entire munitions cabinet. Those that knew anything about weapons saw shotguns, automatic rifles, and even a couple grenades.

"What the hell?" muttered Ron.

"Does anyone think they can run this ship?" asked Max.

Chapter 25

At Max's question, everyone was quiet for a few seconds. Operate the Titanic? The Captain, who presumably knew something about running this ship, hadn't been able to keep it from sinking. What would they do that would be valuable? Nobody volunteered.

Max pursed his lips before asking again, "You don't have to be able to parallel park the damn thing. Can anyone run a ship of any sort?"

"I've owned a couple of yachts," Brad said, "and I grew up going sailing with my granddad. I know the basics."

Now that the ice had been broken, Dennis Fast spoke up as well, "I spent my summers working salvage ships on the bigger rivers and freighters. I wasn't running things, but the captain invited me up to steer on rare occasions. On our expedition, I'd been spending a good bit of time with the captain. He taught me a few things."

"Great," Max answered, tossing them both shotguns. Then he paused for a second. How to explain to these people what they should do? They didn't understand that this world was totally fictional, and he had no desire to share that information with them. They didn't know that what happened here wasn't really happening to actual human beings. And, they could not know. Ever. He'd just have to bluff his way through this.

"You two will be sent back two hours. I want you to shoot your way into the bridge of this ship and take over the controls. Whatever happens, stay in control and do not hit the iceberg. If you don't feel totally capable of operating the ship, think about letting the captain or pilot live. But, order them to alter course so that they avoid the iceberg."

"Wait," Brad said, "rewind a bit. You want us to kill people?"

"Anyone who works on this ship is dead anyways," he said, somewhat proud of the technically accurate, but entirely unclear language. Rachel looked at him and leaned her head to one side, silently judging just how accurately vague he was.

"Not true," Eco retorted in all her literal glory. "Many of the mates helped load boats, then commanded them. You could be killing the wrong people."

Max was losing patience. He had no time for a history lesson from Eco. He just gruffly responded, "Do you all want to live or die? I've no time to argue and debate with you. Just shoot everyone that gets in your way. If *you* want to live, that is our best hope."

Brad Hammer pursed his lips and said, "Can do." He wasn't one to debate smaller points of morality when his own survival was at stake. He'd always wanted to strut around like a badass with a gun. This was his shot.

Now that he'd convinced the first pairing of their task, Max knew his next few assignments would be easier to deliver, "Ron and

Dale, you two will have to search this ship. There's the possibility that a door will be opened somewhere here. If it is you will need to find it, go through, then bring us out."

Happy that they'd not been enlisted to murder or kill as part of their task, Ron and Dale both agreed readily, "Sounds doable."

"It sounds easier than it will be. Remember not to draw too much attention to yourselves in the process. If you get put in the holding tank of the ship by security, we won't be able to get you out. Quest and Zone, you all will look for the door as well. Just break up the floors amongst yourselves, or divide the ship in a way that makes sense to everyone."

"You want us to search this whole ship for a door that may or may not exist?" Zone asked doubtfully, "And we have to hope that in our search we are in the right room at the right time, too…since the door won't stay open for long?"

"You have a better idea there Zone?" Max asked with a degree of fake patience.

"I'm not a quitter. I'm really not," Zone said. "But don't you all think we should start to consider the worst."

"What does that mean?" Quest asked.

"It means that I'd rather go quickly," Zone said holding up a gun rather ominously, "than drown in frigid water."

"Look," Max said, "If you want to shoot yourself, go ahead. No one here will judge you, but I'd rather die trying than die giving up."

Eco tried to talk some sense into Zone, as against her timid nature as lobbying was, "Zone, please don't think that way. We can make this. We've been in sticky situations before and always gotten out. Let's work to find a way out."

"Alright, I was simply mentioning the possibility. I will not drown, but I'll work with you all until it gets to that point."

Max breathed something of a sigh of relief. If Zone had decided to end things in this alternate reality, it would have just as surely killed him back in real life. He was thankful for the help others had provided in talking him down a bit.

"Eco and Becca, now for your assignment. I'm going to send you to a different time."

"What do you mean Max?" Eco replied.

"There may be someone living in the place I sent you that can help us."

"Who is that?" Becca said.

"I wish I knew..." Max trailed off.

"Huh?"

"I don't know who it is, man or woman, young or old, but I'm certain that my father had a fail-safe set somewhere. And, I'm pretty sure I know how to access it. His idea was that, if you ever couldn't get back to home base, you'd go there and the person would reveal themselves."

"How will we know them?"

Max once again paused to consider just how much he should tell them. His motto thus far had been, reveal nothing. It had worked up until this point, kind of, and he decided not to change tactics now.

"I just know they'll reveal themselves. The person will probably be wearing something out of place in their particular time. They may recognize and approach you. I'm not sure how it will work. They may peg you as travelers by what you are wearing."

"How big is this place? If we are dropped in a major city, do we stay put or move around?" Becca pressed for more details. They were going to be sent to a strange place to find a stranger, and they had no way of knowing what sort of person to expect?

"You know what I know," Max replied. "I'm sorry."

"There's nothing else for us to go on?" Eco lamented.

Max did understand how frustrating it would be to be asked to suspend all fears and need for detail. But, he couldn't risk telling them more in front of all these others. Not after what had happened with Baljeet.

"No, I'm sorry, but this is what you need to do. I think Dad would have designed to so that you'll be able to figure it out. I trust that you can both do this together."

"What are you and Rachel going to do?"

"There's one trick I have up my sleeve. I have to try it."

They all looked at each other with frustration etched in each line of their faces. When would he stop being so vague and mysterious?

"Would some specifics, on occasion, really kill you, Max?"

"They might. Here, I got you all some modern day Walkie Talkies...of sorts," Max said as he pulled out tablet computers for each person. "These can communicate through time. We can keep

193

in touch and see each other's progress. And, if one of you find a door, we can all know immediately to get back quickly."

"Can we surf the web on them, boss?" Zone joked.

"Yeah, but the rates are outrageous," Max deadpanned back.

Everyone snickered at the jokes. Dark humor felt therapeutic and welcome.

"Okay, we've all got our assignments. Remember your portion of the plan and stay in touch. We have to be able to keep in contact with each other. We can do this!" he added the last bit of pep, hopeful that he could motivate the others. Max then pushed a few buttons on his computer, and there was the now familiar flash of white light. Instantly, Max, Rachel, Eco, and Becca were gone. The others stood in the same room, but the clock on one wall registered two hours earlier.

"Alright," Ron said, "you all heard him. Let's do this!"

Chapter 26

Not surprisingly, Brad was the first to embrace his new role. He had always been the most callous of Dale's group, and here he was able to embrace both his taste for adventure and his lack of concern for the safety and well-being of others. Even Dennis Fast, who was not the most sensitive or timid of individuals, felt a tinge of revulsion.

Brad turned to Dennis and said eagerly while gesturing to his shotgun, "Let's get to the bridge and see what this thing can do."

Reluctant but resigned, Dennis headed for the door behind Brad. Ron, Dale, Zone and Quest watched as they rushed out. They still needed to divvy up the rooms in the ship.

"I guess we need to decide who goes where," Ron started. "But, does anyone else thing something weird is going on here?"

"I sure do," Dale said.

"It could feel weird since our whole operation has gone to hell in a hand-basket," answered Quest sourly.

"That," Ron nodded, "but something else, too. There is something that Max isn't telling us. I've known him for a long time. And, he can be pretty tough natured. But, I can't imagine him ever telling a guy like Brad Hammer to shoot freely at innocent bystanders."

Quest nodded in agreement. "That's true, but it wasn't what caught *my* attention. I noticed that Max and Rachel somehow changed clothes."

"What do you mean?"

"The clothes they are wearing now are different than the ones in which they arrived. None of the rest of us changed. How did they?"

"That seemed odd to me too, Quest. But, I also noticed when Max got frustrated with us, mumbled about us not 'figuring it out yet.'"

"I'm done trying to figure out much of anything," Zone tried to change the subject, "I just want to get out of here and Max seems to be the only person with any idea of how to do that. I'm just going to follow his instructions. I think you should do the same."

"His instructions are ridiculous..." Ron trailed off. "This ship is massive. Far too massive to achieve what he suggested."

"That's an understatement," Quest said. "Needle in a haystack would be putting it lightly. Let's organize our search to at least give ourselves the best shot at success. How about we start at the bottom fore. You start at the top aft. We meet in the middle. Work for you all?"

"Wait," Dale said. "Remind me what those words mean. My nautical knowledge leaves a bit to be desired."

"Fore is front. Aft is back. Think of words that start with those same prefixes. Forward. Afternoon. After. Forefront. Same concept."

"Gotcha. I'm supposed to start in the front. That is still going to take a lot of time. And, are we expected to search every bit of every room? Every bathroom?"

"And what if doors are locked or people are sleeping?" Zone nodded.

"Well," Quest said, "let's be smart about this. It wouldn't be in one of the smaller sleeper cabins. The doors always happen in open places."

"You hope," Ron said. "But, everything we thought we knew has been thrown on its head."

"I'm trying to be optimistic," Quest answered. "We can't search all the cabins anyways. This really is our only hope."

"Okay," Ron said, "let's just find those doors and get the hell out of here. I may very well retire from Time Vacation when this is all over. That is, if anything is left of the damn place."

#

Up a few flights of stairs, and nearly halfway across the ship, Brad Hammer and Dennis Fast were methodically making their way up to the bridge of the massive ship. They were winded from the exertion and adrenaline that had been coursing through their veins since they left that library. They'd been lucky to find no locked doors on their way upwards and onwards. But, as they came closer to their destination, their run of good luck ebbed in the form of a set of double doors.

"Damn," Brad turned to his partner. "Looks like our string of good fortune is over. This one is locked."

Dennis stood for a second, contemplating what to do in this situation. The doors were symbolic of that old adage about people in the old days making things 'the right way.' They were thick, the hinges were significant, and it looked unlikely to budge even in the face of gunfire. As he wondered what to do next, the answer appeared behind him in the form of approaching footsteps.

Dennis turned to see a younger man in uniform, come around the corner and look towards them suspiciously, "Hey, what are you two doing up here? How did you get here? State your business."

Thinking of the right answer, Dennis stuttered for just a second, "Well...umm."

Suddenly, he was thrust aside by Brad Hammer, who had drawn his shotgun up to firing position.

"BOOOM!!!" The shot echoed in that metal hallway. The crewmember slumped to the floor, blood spreading across his white suit in a growing crimson stain.

"Brad?" Dennis muttered in a mix of frustration and validation. He knew what to expect out of this guy, but was nonetheless disappointed.

"We've got a job to do," Brad replied harshly as he walked over to the mate and took the keys off his belt. "And I'm guessing one of these keys will open this door for us."

"You could have asked him for the keys, Brad. That gun there would have been a pretty powerful argument for him to give them up. There certainly wasn't any need to kill anyone."

"We don't have time and you heard what Max said, Dennis!"

Brad jingled with the keys, searching for the correct one. Finally, he slid a key into the opening, turned it, and the bolt clicked open.

"Got it."

They opened the door slowly, unsure of what might lie ahead but fairly positive the gunfire would have raised an alarm. They made their way around a corner and through an empty room. Finally, they came to another door marked: *No Entry. Ship Personnel Only!*

When Brad peered around the corner of the door, he found a long and narrow hallway.

"Come on," he urged Dennis.

Together they walked that hallway to another door, this time a single. It wasn't locked, and when they swung it open three guys turned quickly and defensively to see who was there. When they saw Dennis and Brad, the one wearing a sidearm on his hip reached for it. Without thinking much about the options, Dennis shot him. As that shot echoed, the other two guys reached for something under the counter. Brad shot the one to the right directly in the chest. Shotguns don't need great aim to hit hard. These guys were like fish in a barrel. Upon seeing his two colleagues gunned down, the third crewmember froze and stopped reaching for whatever it was under the counter.

"Don't move," Brad said ominously, "unless you want to join your mates here."

Dennis turned back to the door through which they'd just entered and went back to lock it. For good measure, he also put a big chair in front. They didn't have the only keys on board this massive boat, and if someone else came through they'd want a bit of time to react. Brad had turned his attentions to the controls of the ship, and as he looked over the complexity and breadth of buttons, levers, and gauges, he was really quite happy that he'd kept one of these guys around to help.

"More here to fool with than those yachts I'm used to," he mumbled to Dennis.

"All we really need is the speed and wheel controls," Dennis replied. "You!" he turned to the guard. "We need to know how to turn this thing and how to make speed up and slow down. If you won't help us with that, we don't really have much of a reason to keep you around."

The lone surviving mate looked at the guns Dennis and Brad held in their hands and stuttered a bit, "Uh…well…I can show you."

"He can't help us with the biggest problem, though," Brad looked to Dennis. "How do we avoid the berg?"

"I'd say we just steer around it," Brad argued.

The nervous mate looked from Brad to Dennis as they spoke. He had no idea what they were talking about, or what particular iceberg they referenced, but he was eager to be of assistance if it would save his life.

"Problem is," Dennis said, "How to do that without hitting another one. It isn't like there is just one iceberg in these waters."

Brad agreed, "Yeah. You are right. But, we know the current course does not end well. So, we either turn north or south."

"What do you think?" Dennis asked.

"Let's go south," Brad answered, "Just turn straight south and see where that takes us."

"I guess it is as good a choice as any," Dennis conceded, "At least it can't work out worse."

As he turned to carry out their plan, a sound behind them started both of these new navigators. They turned to find another shipmate barging into the office, prepared for conflict. He must have seen the fallen bodies of his friends in the hallway, and had a gun ready. But, he didn't account for the fact that there would be an additional obstacle in the way. He was halfway through the door when it's progress was hindered by the chair. It slowed him just enough to let Dennis and Brad turn and shoot. He fell through the doorway dead. His shipmate, the one who'd been standing quietly, foolishly decided that this was his chance to reach for a hidden gun. Brad saw him as he moved and shot him too. Now, these two unprepared time travelers were all alone with the ship's controls.

Brad turned to Dennis again, "Still south?"

"Aye," Dennis agreed. "Full steam."

Brad grabbed the wheel of the ship and started to turn it to the left. He watched a center dial in front of him shift, as the arrow started to move from NW to S. The ship listed a bit, enough for anyone on board to have felt it, as they turned. With that turn, Dennis and Brad knew that they could expect more visitors soon. The ship's captain would wonder why in the hell his boat had turned during the middle of the night. He'd be up to check soon. But, not soon enough. Because, just as soon as that arrow hit the letter S, a flash of light flickered through the room.

"What the hell?" Brad squinted his eyes.

"Another time jump," Dennis replied knowingly. "Brace yourself."

#

Down a few levels of the ship, as they searched the gathering rooms, stairwells, and common spaces, Ron, Dale, Quest, and Zone met each other in the hallway after half an hour of fruitless searching.

"No luck?" Ron asked the others.

"Nothing," the all conceded.

"Maybe we ought to stick together for the time being just in case something happens. I've got some sort of feeling…" Dale said.

"Anyone looked at their tablets for news from the others?"

"Nope," Quest said as he pulled out his computer to do just that. Before he could get it out of his bag, though, a flash of white forecast to them yet another jump.

Chapter 27

Max may not have been able to predict where they were going to end up, but Eco and Becca had luckily appeared in an amazing and tranquil site. They stood on a well-trod pathway, but signs of human traffic thick enough to have formed this path were nowhere to be seen. They stood all alone on this path, looking both directions. Everything about this place was a reversal of where they'd come from. On the ship, it had been night and winter. Here, it seemed to be the first hint of morning. A few brave leaves were clinging tightly to the branches of massive trees overhead, the oranges and reds a vivid visual cue of a season ending.

To the right, the path stretched a couple hundred yards into the distance, generally keeping a straight course under a massive canopy of spruce, pine, and oaks. Eco started down the path towards the left, which curved over a slight incline and out of sight. Becca followed close behind.

"Why this way?" she asked.

"It isn't really the road not taken. But, I can't see where this end goes…seems a bit more fun to me!"

They made their way over the incline and saw below them, along the path, a quaint, little, trickling stream. Someone years past had even constructed a little curved footbridge. They walked over it and back up towards a brighter area of the woods. As they neared that brightness, a clearing came into view. Not much requiring sun would have grown in that forest, but enough sun came through the clearing to sustain a tangle of pumpkin vines. Along those vines grew the most massive orange pumpkins that Becca or Eco had ever seen.

"Beautiful!" Becca gasped.

"Reminds me of Halloween as a kid," Eco replied. "I was a scarecrow a couple years in a row. I loved the *Wizard of Oz!*"

As she said it, she motioned towards the scarecrow that stood guard over this patch of pumpkins, dissuading any animals or varmints from getting too comfortable raiding the garden.

"What country do you think we are in?" Eco asked. "What time period?"

"I have no idea. But, if I see Ichabod Crane, I'm running!" Becca joked.

"Huh?"

"Nothing. Just a story I read as a kid."

Eco thought distantly for a second, but nothing came to her, "I think we need to find some shelter by the end of the day. These woods are nicer during dawn than they would be during dusk."

"I'd imagine that someone lives relatively close, given this pumpkin patch. Want to split up, head in opposite directions, and then meet back here in an hour?" Becca asked.

"That won't be necessary," came a soft voice from behind them.

Both Becca and Eco nearly jumped out of their skin as they turned to see the owner of it. They were both relieved to see a petite, and stunningly beautiful, young woman. She had long black hair, skin like something out of a Mediterranean epic poem, and full lips.

"Shit!" Eco said. "What in the world? How did you walk up right behind us without us hearing?"

"I live here. I know every stick and leaf. I can be quiet if the occasion merits it."

Becca looked her over. She was like some image from National Geographic. She wore a light blue silk dress that hung over every curve perfectly. It was like something a princess would wear on casual occasions, and had obviously been specifically tailored to her figure. She wore turquoise bangles on her wrists, a matching stone around her neck, and even had a little golden stud in her nose.

"Who are you?" Becca asked.

"I'm Tia."

"Are you who were are supposed to be looking for."

"Well, I'm the only one here. So, if you are looking for someone else you might find yourself frustrated."

"I'm Becca and this is Eco. We are pleased to meet you. Do you know what we are supposed to do here?"

"I can create a door. I am programmed to create doors."

"Programmed? What are you talking about?" Eco was confused. That word was so specific, and it had such specific connotations for her. She hadn't heard it much other than in a software class she took senior year of college. *Programmed?*

Tia either did not understand that Eco was asking about the word choice, or she was blatantly ignoring it, "My first function is to create doors."

"You have other functions too?" Becca asked.

"Yes, but I cannot perform those functions with you."

"With whom do you perform your other functions with?"

"Only Maximilian."

Eco looked at Becca, now totally lost, "Where did he send us?"

"I don't know," Becca answered, "but at least she can help us." Becca turned to Tia. "Will you create a door to get us out of here?"

"Yes, if Max comes to join you. I only perform for Maximilian. It is my function. No one else. Only him."

"What the hell?" Eco stomped off a few feet to take a deep breath, "So Tia, who only performs for Max, what do you suggest we do?"

"Wait for Maximilian to arrive."

"How does he do that?" Becca asked.

"We must go to my house. That is where he comes for me."

"What is this place?" Eco asked. "Where is this place? What country is this? What year is it?"

"Country? Year?" Tia said confused. "This is my home. I live here. I don't know what you mean by year or country."

Becca looked at Tia's confused expression and tried to clarify, "Does anyone else live in your homeland, Tia?"

"There is no one else here. I have never met other humans before except for you. Maximilian comes to visit me."

"What do you all do when he visits?"

"We take walks down this road. There's a pond down the way. We have lunch there and go swimming in it. We talk and enjoy ourselves."

"Is that it?" Eco asked somewhat maliciously.

"No, that is not it. There are other things, but I'm not permitted to talk about those things with anyone else."

"How old are you, Tia? How long have you lived here?"

"Old?" She said absently. It wasn't that Tia seemed obstinate or mean. She either had no idea what they were talking about or was fabulous at acting.

"This is so weird," Eco said to Becca.

"Follow me," Tia said, ignoring Eco's comment.

Tia started off down the path and Becca turned towards Eco.

"Weird, indeed." Then, her voice went to a whisper, "It's like she is not really a human being, but she looks the part. Well, looks the part of a supernaturally attractive human being. I don't get it."

Tia led them on a leisurely walk. She stopped a couple times to pick some berries off bushes growing near the path. She put them in a hand-woven bag over her shoulder as the other two women watched in wonder. About five minutes into their journey, Tia took a few steps off the path and bent down. She carefully pulled up a plant with green leaves and a subtle white blossom, taking care to obtain the root of this plant as well as the stem.

"Garlic?" Becca asked.

"Yes," Tia replied. "One of my other functions is cooking for Maximilian. He likes it when I cook."

"Well," Eco said, "if this is another world...at least it still has the familiar stench of chauvinism."

Tia looked almost through Eco as she said it. She didn't reply, instead turned and walked on. After another five minutes or so, they made their way into another clearing, this one much broader. The two women looked out over a small lake, which sat next to a quaint cabin.

Becca spoke about the scene first, "Wait. Isn't that..."

"Just like Max's cabin?" Eco finished the thought.

"Yeah."

"You've been to Max's cabin?" Eco asked.

"Yeah, he's had that place for ages. Sarah would have me up for long weekends there. We'd read and sip wine out on the dock."

"So, it wasn't filled with computers and time-travel pods when you were there?"

"No," Becca answered. "He must have added that later. I haven't been up there for years."

"This experience just gets weirder and weirder."

They walked down a cobblestoned path to a door opposite the lake. Tia opened it and walked inside. She made her way over to a counter and put down her bag, starting to pull from it the fruits of her walk. Becca and Eco looked around the room. Whereas Eco's impression of Max's cabin was of a new-age time travel, this one was rustic. In the corner sat a bookshelf with a few dusty volumes.

There was a sofa and a matching leather chair, each worn with age. A stone fireplace was on the left wall, and what looked to be last night's embers gleamed faintly with leftover heat.

"I don't understand, Tia." Becca said.

Tia looked to her in total confusion, "There is nothing to understand. Everything just is. That's what the creator says."

"The creator?" Eco asked, though she was starting to get an inkling as to how Tia might answer that question.

"Of course. The creator. Maximilian Blank."

Chapter 28

Max and Rachel had returned to a now familiar site, and the luxurious hotel was every bit as busy as she remembered it. They made their way through the lobby to the elevator. Rachel stood quietly as Max pressed the "Penthouse" button once inside and the doors had closed, waited for it to arrive at that destination, and followed him quietly down the hall. He produced a key from his pants pocket and led her inside.

"I need to think…" Max said almost to himself. "Got to figure some things out. Need to think…"

Rachel just watched him as he made his way to the stainless fridge in the kitchen, "Beer?" he asked her absently as he opened the door.

"Yes, please."

Max rummaged through a drawer, looking for a bottle opener. Upon finding it, he opened the two frosty bottles he'd pulled out. Max handed Rachel one. She sat in the chair opposite the couch into which Max slumped in an air of fatigue.

"Does something seem off to you?" he asked Rachel.

"Max, I can't even begin to answer that question. Everything about this experience now seems off. I have no damn idea what is going on."

"Something is off. I'm not sure. I didn't put it together when you first said the names."

"What names?"

"Dale and Brad."

"So?" Rachel asked taking her first drink of the perfectly chilled beer.

"The names together didn't catch my ear. But, when I saw them together it was like some bell chimed in my distant memory."

"What are you thinking?"

"They were the two that helped finance the board."

"What board?"

"The board that took the company out of my hands. After Dad died. They were the ring leaders of that group."

"Okay, but neither of them seem to like Ron very much. Why would they have made him CEO?"

"Maybe Dale thought that Ron could be bought. I don't know. That was a misjudgment though for sure. The man is nothing if not principled. Slightly dense, yes. A poor businessman, sure. Dishonest? No. Maybe he thought that Ron would help him search for treasure, but Ron actually developed a sense of loyalty to the business and didn't want to risk the company."

"That could be true…" Rachel agreed.

"I don't know how to explain it. Another thing: Baljeet could not have been killed just from jumping. It doesn't work that way. Someone had to have killed him during the jump. Or maybe right before everyone else arrived in that room. Sometimes, when you know the system, you can rig it so that people arrive slightly later than you did. They don't notice the difference."

"Someone in our group killed Baljeet?"

"Yeah, I think so."

"And you think that Dale or Brad had something to do with it?"

"Well, it doesn't make any sense to me for them to have been involved in his death. After all, the recruited him to help with the search for those ships. They seemed to have gotten along."

"Maybe they had a falling out?" Rachel asked.

"I don't think so. We would have noticed tensions between them. Baljeet wasn't very good at keeping a poker face."

Max nodded deep in thought. "Baljeet was just a pawn. He wasn't involved in any way with ownership or Time Vacation policy. Nobody should have cared enough to kill him. I don't get it. But, I've got help on the way."

"Help?" Rachel asked.

Just then, a door opened to reveal Shawn, Lacey, and Heidi. They were all wearing the bikinis that they'd worn the last time Rachel saw them.

"Hey, Max," Rachel laughed. "I mean, I understand, but every woman in this system is hot and often near naked. Think you might have a bit of an obsession? You know that women often wear real clothes when they aren't at the pool?"

Max laughed as the other three girls glared at Rachel in angry confusion. Both Lacey and Heidi looked down at their bodies and tied the robes they had previously had loosely over their shoulders to cover up a bit more.

213

"Don't listen to her!" Max said to them all, "We'll talk her into that attire choice at some point. Until then, have a seat my lovelies."

"You need information?" Shawn asked Max.

"I do, Shawn. During a jump, something happened. One of our people died. I need to know how."

"Okay," Shawn replied. As she nodded in agreement, into her hand flashed a remote control. It was just...not there and then it was. The only person that would have been surprised by this capacity to manifest needed objects directly from the system—Rachel—wasn't watching. She was looking towards the television, which Shawn soon turned on. She flipped a couple channels, went past her destination, then flipped back. "Here it is."

On the screen flashed a room in a ship that looked familiar to Rachel. Within seconds, Baljeet and Zone entered the room in a flash of light.

"Where are the others?" Baljeet looked to Zone in confusion. He'd never seen the system jump people at different times.

"They'll be a few more minutes." Zone asked.

"Why are they slower?"

"You don't know, old man?" Zone asked.

Baljeet had in him none of the bitterness that now oozed from Zone with each word. He was slow to notice it in his colleague as well.

"Know what, Zone?"

"Time travel. This whole business to which you've devoted your life, and that you betrayed for money. It is all a sham."

"What do you mean?" Baljeet asked.

"Time travel is impossible. This is all virtual reality."

Baljeet looked down to his hands, turning them palm side up. He balled them both into fists, observing the mystery and perfect synchronicity of those muscle movements.

"Impossible," he said, almost as a conclusion.

"I really don't have time, or the inclination, to convince you," Zone said. "And it is probably a more sure fire success this way."

As he did so, he walked over to Baljeet, grabbed him by the shoulders, and aggressively turned him around. Then, Zone reached up to put his arm around the frail Indian man who was too surprised to anticipate anything malicious. By the time Baljeet realized he should resist, Zone had him in tight choke hold.

As Baljeet struggled for breath, Zone whispered into his ear, "This isn't your fault. It really isn't, but everyone is going to pay. I helped invent this system. I was Dan's top guy. I had a wonderful job. Then, he dies and I'm stuck working as an underpaid stiff."

Baljeet was fading, and was trying to whisper something without the necessary breath. Zone didn't let up, "They promised me great wealth. But then, Ron came and messed everything up!"

Zone took great satisfaction as he ranted about life's inequities, in the feeling of Baljeet slumping more and more into oblivion. Finally, someone was feeling the pain he'd felt all those years working a dead-end job. Finally, someone else was reaping the punishment they'd long deserved.

Baljeet's eyes, which Max and the ladies could see on the TV screen, were filled with terror. He was terrified of death, and certainly was not thinking of the fact that this was virtual reality and not the real world.

Zone whispered into his ear, "You were just a bit unlucky, old man. Unlucky. I have my plan. Killing you was part of it, but don't take it too personally. You won't be the last."

At that moment, Zone relaxed his chokehold and stepped away from Baljeet's body. Ron, Dale, Dennis, Quest, and Eco flashed into the room.

"What happened?" Ron asked when he saw Baljeet lying on the floor.

In an amazing display of acting, Zone said innocently, "I don't know. He was on the floor when I got here."

Chapter 29

The three beautiful women seemed entirely unfazed by what they'd just seen, as if they were watching a rerun of some episode to a television crime drama. They knew the ending, so they were not surprised when it happened. Heidi leaned into Lacey, her hand draped just close enough to her breast to remind Rachel that a man had programed them. The only guy in the room, though, was too preoccupied to notice. Rachel, too, previously so obsessed with the beauty and mannerisms of these women, sat on the deep couch staring at the now blank TV screen in absolute shock. Her mouth was gaped open but no sound escaped. Here, in this Virtual Reality, there had been a genuine murder. The change in Zone was shocking. She'd really not noticed much in his mannerisms that suggested he was capable of such things. She looked over to Max to see what he had to say about this revelation. His lips were placed together tightly, his eyes were squinting just a bit, and he was nodding slowly.

"Max? Penny for your thoughts."

"Huh?" he startled at her question.

"What are you thinking?"

"I'm thinking that I should have known, Rachel."

"About Zone?"

"Yeah, none of what he told Baljeet was news to me. I knew that he'd been pissed when Ron took over. And, he might have overplayed how important he was to Dad's research, but he was incredibly valuable to several of major developments. I can see why he thought he should have been first in line to run to place. It wasn't my call, so I didn't think much of it, but his grievances are based on genuine slights."

"But, do you think he'd want to kill all of us?" Rachel asked, "If he had such loyalty towards your Dad?"

"Maximilian, honey," Lacey interjected, "can I offer an explanation?"

"Sure," Max replied, wondering at the same time why he hadn't asked these women before now.

"Well, Zone enlisted Dennis in creating the story about the ships and treasure. They knew that Dale and Brad would be interested. They also knew about the tension between Dale and Brad and Ron."

"Zone and Dennis are brothers," Shawn interrupted.

Lacey nodded, "Yes. They worked through this together. They intended to kill Dale, Brad, and Ron in the system. They didn't count on Ron bringing you in to this whole thing. Zone was going to make sure that Becca, Quest, and Eco got out safely."

"But, Time Vacation would have been blamed..." Max said, "and neither Dennis nor Zone would get what they wanted anyway. I'm unclear about their intentions."

"Not true," Lacey argued. "Ancient Recovery would have been blamed for not running the system safely. You would be forced to come back to run the company."

"So, he did all of this…for me?" Max muttered.

Shawn shook her head, "I don't know that I'd go that far. He did it for himself too. If you were forced back, he would have been one of your first calls, right?"

"Yes," Max agreed. "Certainly."

"His position would have been infinitely better with you there, so he didn't just do it out of the goodness of his heart."

"But why did Dale and Brad oust Max and bring Ron in in the first place?" Rachel asked trying to wrap her head around all of this.

"My guess," Lacey said tilting her head causing her to appear deep in thought, "Dale and Brad thought Ron would allow them to use the perceived time travel system to find hidden treasure. They would become richer and more famous."

"How do you know all of that? What people are thinking—their motives?" Rachel asked Lacey.

"Maximilian has me monitor everything that happens. It helps when you can see everyone's actions, then go back and watch those of the others. Perspective becomes a lot clearer that way. I also watched what Baljeet and Dale were doing. I reasoned from there. I could be off."

"You can think? Artificial intelligence?"

Heidi leaned up from the couch to answer, "We can reason, not think."

"I don't know that I follow the difference," Rachel said confused.

"It's like plugging a math formula into a computer," Max said.

"Go on..." Rachel said.

"Well, the computer can't come up with the formula. But, once you've put it into the system, it'll work related problems more quickly than humans can."

Rachel ignored her additional questions and instead pushed the conversation towards some sort of conclusion.

"Well, now that we have an idea about Zone's motives, what do we do with that information?"

Max nodded in agreement, "Should we leave without doing anything to stop him, or intervene?"

"Who says you have to leave," Heidi said as she leaned over and rested her hands provocatively on his knee. "Stay here with us. We could make you..." she paused for effect, "very happy."

As if to demonstrate one element of what she meant, Heidi leaned over and kissed Max deeply. As she did so, she ran her hands up his leg just enough to convey very clearly her meaning. At that, Rachel decided that she'd intervene before this developed past the point of appropriate. She leaned over, pulled Heidi's gently but firmly hand off Max, and coughed loudly enough to distract them both. They stopped kissing and looked at Rachel as she cleared her throat.

"Excuse me, you two. Max, come with me."

Rachel led him into the bedroom next to the living area, walked him over to the bed, and directed him to take a seat. Max raised his hand to indicate, just a second. Then he walked over to the sink in the bathroom and turned on the sink. He looked into the mirror as he waited for the water to heat. Then, he splashed some three times in his face. As it dripped off, he looked up again towards the mirror, as if he was searching somehow internally for the answers to these questions that plagued him.

"Max, come sit down," Rachel said as she patted the bed next to her.

He walked across the room and did as commanded. He bent over slightly with the weight of choices.

"Max, look at this place," Rachel started.

"What do you mean? I've seen it. I've probably spent more time here than I have in the real world over the last ten years."

"Why don't we stay?"

"Huh?"

"I mean. Could we? Stay here. Have the perfect life?"

"It's not perfect. Trust me."

"Why not? Any man I know would consider that out there," she motioned towards the three lovelies who now had their ears to the door, "pretty close to perfect."

"That out there," Max nodded, "is awesome."

"I'm sure," Rachel laughed.

Max paused and thought before continuing, "For a while. But, it isn't sustainable because it's not real. It never will be, and we will always know that."

"But to think, anything we want. Never to worry again." Rachel said almost lustily. "How long could we live here, Max?"

"It doesn't matter."

"Think about it. We could have kids here and never have to change a diaper.

Never have to worry about a temper tantrum. They'll turn out perfect."

"But they won't be real. Trust me, Rachel. Not to mention the problems with perfection."

"What do you mean?"

"The diapers…they are a great example. Kids are messy. They stink. They poop their pants and pee on you when you are changing them."

"Yeah, but not here!" Rachel urged.

"When you lose that stuff, Rachel, it isn't the same. The sweets eventually aren't as sweet without the bitter. It's a cliché, but to have a full understanding of light you need to also know dark."

"You don't think we've had enough dark in our lives by now to relish perfection for a while?" Rachel asked.

"No, it gets old quick. I've been there. I'd rather have a million heartbreaks than to never be able to feel one again. Without the capacity for loss and tragedy, positives are hollow and shallow. It gets old too quickly."

"What got old to you?" Rachel pressed for proof.

"I had everything. Everything here a person could ever want. You've seen the women. This hotel. There are plenty of amazing sites that you haven't seen, too. Lived in castles, mansions, cabins on the most pristine and beautiful lakes, and also the ones with the best fishing. I've watched the most beautiful sunsets you've ever seen over beaches and mountain tops."

"This is the problem you were describing?" Rachel scoffed.

Max continued, "And I partied like a rock star, knowing that nothing I did would ever affect me, but it did. After a while you can't feel anything anymore. The drugs, the booze, the women, hell, even fishing gets boring when there's no challenge. Trust me when I say this Rachel, this is not the life you want. I know that it isn't the one I want."

"I can't believe you would give this all up."

"It was the best thing that I ever did. I had lost my way. Didn't know who I was. Finally, and I think I got the strength from memories of Sarah, I summoned up the courage to leave it behind."

"And the girls out there?

"They could do things that you can't even imagine. And, that was great for a while. But, once again, it's not real. It's like knowing that you're in a dream. You can create anything, but it's not real. Nothing you do here matters. It makes no difference if you live like a king or a bum."

"When was the last time you were in here?"

"It's been a couple of years now. But, to them it was yesterday. The first weeks without were hardest. I was like an addict. But, eventually the temptation receded. And, I felt so much better with each day out."

Rachel was not yet ready to give up, "But think of all the things we could do here..."

"I won the Super Bowl, pitched Game 7 of the World Series, played goalie in the Stanley Cup, and won the Ultimate Fighting Championship in the same day. I had all three of those women out there that night. I know well the things we can do. But, it isn't real. It does not matter. The feeling of all that stuff pales in comparison to a real eighth grader's first kiss or a high school quarterback winning a local playoff game. Without real consequences and friends validating successes, they don't matter."

"I still think I'd like to give it a try. But, I'll trust you Max. If you don't want to stay, though...what do we do now?"

"First I need to say goodbye to them." He motioned once more to the three women. "You seem to be imagining how great it would be here. But, you probably can't imagine how hard it was to walk out of here. To walk away from the best dreams you've ever had."

"I'm not telling you we have to," Rachel replied testily.

"I know, but we must. We have to find the key."
"Key?"

The doorway out. Only one knows it. That's where I sent Eco and Becca. The system is on a different server so the jumps won't affect it. They should have made contact with the key holder, by now."

Rachel smiled slyly, "Call me crazy, but why do I get the feeling that the key holder is easy on the eyes?"

Max just smiled, "not sure, dad created that one."

"And the others? The ones back on the ship?" Rachel asked.

"If Zone and Dennis did come here to kill the others, we should stop them." Max conceded almost reluctantly.

"Should?"

Max looked away from Rachel, got up off the couch, and began to pace the room. He looked like Rachel felt before getting out of the car and walking into the dentist's office.

"I suppose we need to do the right thing."

Rachel laughed at Max, "Well, you don't sound very enthused about it."

"That makes sense since I'm not. I mean, I really don't care two cents for some of them. I'd be fine with going and getting Quest, Eco and Becca, then heading out. But, the rest of them shouldn't die in here."

Rachel looked at Max and thought of disagreeing. It seemed like a couple those people very much deserved whatever fate befell them. As she considered explaining all of those deaths to her boss' back home, though, she reconsidered her position. She'd been sent here on a mission, and she was not someone who liked to leave tasks undone.

"Let's go," Max said as he headed towards the door.

"Do you want me to wait in here while you tell them goodbye?"

"I was actually wondering," Max paused as if to consider the wisdom of what he was about to say, "If you might say goodbye with me to them…in here?"

Rachel processed what he meant, then slapped him playfully on the arm, "Not a chance, Romeo."

Max shrugged his shoulders, "It was certainly worth a shot!"

His laughter stopped short as he opened the door and the three women he'd just referenced nearly fell forward. They'd been listening, and wore sad expressions on each of their beautiful faces.

"Is what we've just heard true Max?"

"Yes, I'm afraid it is."

"What will that mean for us?" Heidi asked.

"It really does not mean much. You won't feel a thing. But, this is goodbye. For good."

"Will you not take any of us with you?" Shawn pleaded.

"I can't. I wish I could. But, I just cannot do that," Max said apologetically.

"Then Max," Lacey said first, "I love you."

"I love you too, Max," Shawn added.

"Me too…" Heidi said as the tenderest tear slid down her blushing cheek. Her doe eyes looked positively tragic as she cried.

Max was torn. He knew that he should have been moved by their emotions. And, it felt so good to have these physical and audible manifestations of affection. It felt fulfilling in some way to have people tell him these things, to know that they'd miss him. But, he also knew that they'd been programed to play this particular part. He knew that there was no flesh form that actually felt those tears, this sadness, other than him. He knew that, as soon as he exited this realm of virtual space, these women would cease to exist, that they'd feel nothing as they disappeared into the depths of the technological ether.

"Goodbye, girls."

He pulled out his tablet computer, hit the button on the upper left corner, and started working feverishly. Once he'd punched a few buttons, he looked to Rachel.

"Grab my arm," he instructed.

She did so, and she leaned in a bit more closely than was necessary. Perhaps she wanted to affirm that, as he left this created dream world, he did so with a companion beside him. Perhaps she was just scared. That was the thing with real people...you could never know for sure their intentions. As Max contemplated all of these things, a flash of light struck and they were gone. In that instant, the virtual reality he'd so painstakingly created and perfected years earlier began to crumble. Neither Lacey, nor Heidi, nor Shawn flinched or cried out as they were crushed under the rubble of a previously luxurious hotel. They vanished without pain or emotion and were gone.

Chapter 30

Maximilian Blank was not the only one saying his goodbyes in those fateful hours. And, his goodbyes were not the only sort of farewell occurring at that time either. In fact, his bore very little similarity to the angry disputes in that other time and place of the virtual system.

Another room was empty for a brief second before six men flashed into it. It had the tiny holes characteristic of a ship, but those windows were covered by lengthy velvet curtains. A crystal chandelier glimmered in the darkness, providing the only light. For the few that didn't know they were in a virtual system rather than a real time-rollercoaster, things had become so disorienting that any effort to unlock the mysteries had long-since ceased.

After this latest abrupt jump, they landed with Dale, Brad, Quest, and Ron on one side of the room near a small bookshelf. Across from them stood Zone and Dennis.

"Where are we now?" Ron asked in frustration.

"Same ship, I think…" Quest replied.

"This is the room we jumped into originally you morons," Zone said angrily.

At the precise moment that ship struck something big.

Boom! The sound of the blow rang throughout the ship, and was followed by some significant creaks and shudders.

"The berg! We've hit the iceberg!" Dale said. "Looks like Dennis and Brad were unsuccessful in their mission."

"We got interrupted a bit prematurely!" Brad protested.

The group braced themselves against the walls or furniture nearby until the shaking subsided as nearly as quickly as it had started.

"This could work," Dale said.

"What do you mean?"

"When we jumped in here originally, a door showed up. Maybe another one should appear here soon."

Everyone in the group, save Dennis, was watching Dale try to explain how their exit was going to soon appear. With their eyes on him, no one saw as Zone turned towards the gun cabinet in the closet behind him and picked up one of the shotguns. No one even noticed as he took five shells and slid them into the chamber, each entering with a distinct metallic click. No one except Dennis, who was angling over towards his brother to pick up some ammunition for his gun. Before he'd reached the cabinet, though, a *whisk* sound sounded and a doorway appeared just as Dale had foretold. Unfortunately for most of the travelers, as that door appeared Zone jumped right between it and them. It was only then that they noticed he was holding a gun and aiming it at their heads. To their left, Dennis picked up another gun leisurely and walked over towards Zone. He too aimed his gun right at them.

He disarmed Brad first and foremost, "Mr. Hammer, I'll take that weapon if you don't mind."

"What the hell are you doing, Dennis? Zone?"

"Shut up, Ron. I really can't stand to hear you talk anymore."

"What?"

"Wait just a second, will ya?" Zone said angrily.

Everyone sat quietly until, to their chagrin and great fear, the door behind Dennis and Zone disappeared.

"What's going on here?" Dale broke the silence.

"What's going on, Dale, should not be so far beyond your comprehension. But, the feebleness of your mind never ceases to amaze. So, I'll explain it for you."

"Please do, because we just missed our last escape option." Dale replied.

"I'll start at the beginning. We have time," Zone shot back. "I had a great job within Time Management. Upper management. It paid well. Enough to pay for a hefty mortgage and send my kids to private school, too."

"Okay..." Ron invited him to continue, still baffled about the point.

"But, then you all," he glared at Dale, Brad, and Ron, "took over the company. And I was out. I lost my home. I lost my family; my wife left, taking my kids. Speaking of my kids...they haven't seen me in two years because I lost the custody battle."

Ron disagreed, "I didn't want this, Zone. I wanted to run the company as a professional business. Dale and Brad were the ones that wanted to cheat history."

"We wanted to bring history to the masses," Dale shot back snarkily.

Ron was shaking his head in disagreement from the moment Dale began speaking, "Bullshit. You wanted to make money."

"Shut up! All of you!" Dennis yelled.

"Ron, I don't care about these internal disputes you have with Brad and Dale. I care that I was passed over for promotion time and time again, even though I was clearly the most qualified person there. I care that you ignored me because you were threatened by my experience."

"Zone, I wish I'd known," Ron said quietly. "It never occurred to me that…"

"Of course it didn't. Just shut it, will you. I need to think for a second." Zone turned to Dennis, "Watch them."

Zone walked over and sat on one of the chairs nearby. He wanted to tell these men that they'd been fighting over a system of which they didn't have the slightest understanding. He wanted to tell them they were morons. He wanted to smile as he explained to them that they'd never traveled through time, and that they'd been participants in the most sophisticated and realistic virtual reality system ever created. He wanted Ron to feel just how shallow and fake his entire existence had been since he'd taken over Time Vacation. But he was bound to a deeper and more virulent set of desires, too. He wanted, most of all, to kill all of these men.

These contrasting desires posed a problem for him. If he succumbed to his first set of desires, and told them that they'd been in a land of make-believe and not real time travel, he ran a very real risk. If he told them this was fake, and they believed it deeply enough, they might just survive. He'd never seen it before, and Max was convinced that knowledge of the Virtual system couldn't save you from death inside it. But, Zone didn't want to take any chances. Above all else, he wanted to kill the sons of bitches that ruined his career, his family, his entire universe.

He stood resolutely with a plan and spoke, "Alright, you three. I'm not going to spoil the surprise of this place. I'll let you wonder. But, you should and can know one thing: there were never any ships. No treasure, Dale."

"What are you talking about?" Dale said, "We had the books. We know that treasure existed. We just needed to wait a bit more on that island."

"No!" Zone yelled vehemently, almost losing his cool enough to spill the proverbial beans. "You are wrong! We faked all of it. All of that stuff was completely bogus. Dennis and I knew exactly how to bring the *great* Dale Brooks and Brad Hammer in."

"I don't understand what you mean," Brad muttered.

"You want to know what we relied upon Brad?"

"I guess so, though I'm unclear what you are talking about."

"We used your own greed! You two couldn't stand to let a treasure pass you by, even though everyone involved tried to convince you that it was dangerous and could harm other people. You don't care enough about other people for that to work. You care only for your selfish selves!"

"Listen, Zone," Ron started.

"And you!" Zone shouted. "Shut up too! You should have promoted me ages ago. Going to work was a daily insult to my intelligence and history, and if you'd thought for one second beyond your own ego you would have understood that!"

"We can work this out, Zone," Ron tried to persuade him. Zone just shook his head maliciously.

Quest, who'd previously been quiet, finally pleaded, "What did I do?"

"Wrong place, wrong time," Zone said without any emotion in his voice. "Just like Baljeet."

Quest looked down towards the floor, and as he did so he noticed that his hands were shaking uncontrollably. He'd never been the bravest person, but this external manifestation of fear was slightly embarrassing. Finally, Dennis spoke up, eager to claim his stake of credit in the project the two had painstakingly planned.

"My brother and I knew this would work. We didn't expect Ron to bring Max in, but he's on his own now. Baljeet knew too much so he had to go. And now the rest of you must die."

"Wait," Brad urged, "you can't do this."

"Can't do it?" Dennis scoffed. "You didn't seem so reluctant with a shotgun in your hands just a half hour earlier. You blasted anyone in your way. I wonder what you'd have done if those people had actually hurt your livelihood?"

"But I..." Brad stuttered.

"Enough," Zone glared at each of them as he slid the trigger lock of his Beretta shotgun. The ship, as he said that, listed over to the side. Screams echoed all over the ship as passengers began to grow more frantic. Because those passengers were screaming, no one but Dennis and Zone heard the gunshots ring out. Where there once were six, now stood only two.

"Now," Dennis said, unshaken by the four murders in which he'd just partaken, "How the hell do we get out of here good brother?"

"I put a trace on Max. Where he is, that is where we will appear."

"Great," Dennis said.

"Let's bring a couple of those handguns just in case," Zone said as he pulled his bag off his shoulder and reached in for the computer.

"You got it," Dennis said as he went to the gun-closet and started rummaging through it.

Zone started to punch a few buttons, then paused for Dennis to join him.

"Make sure you hold on to me, now," he told his brother, "and be ready for anything. I'd like it if the others could live, but it doesn't matter nearly as much to me as our own well-being."

With that malicious and selfish statement, both Zone and Dennis disappeared from the Titanic mirage with a flash of light, leaving behind them the bodies of Ron, Dale, Brad, and Quest. Their physical forms, back in the real world, had died at precisely the same moment that they'd been shot. They were too convinced of their own deaths to survive.

Chapter 31

It had been a while since Max had visited, but he knew which direction to walk once he and Rachel appeared on the same path that, hours earlier, Becca and Eco had traversed. They walked over the delightful little creek, past the pumpkin patch, and towards the cabin. Rachel marveled at just how perfectly the details of this place were created. It reminded her of the North Carolina Smokey Mountains during early October—her father had always taken the family on a trip during the fall. It was his favorite season.

"It's just a bit further over this bend," Max told her. "I'm shocked that it's here though; I never knew…I never knew that dad knew about this place I mean."

"I'm in no hurry Max. This is lovely!"

"Well, we really should not take our time. The others on the Titanic don't have tons of time."

"Right." They came around the bend and looked down on the cabin.

"Look familiar?" Max said playfully.

"Of course," she said. "Run out of places to create?"

"Some places are so good," Max answered, "that you don't need to change much. I just added a dimension or two here."

Rachel wondered what he meant by that. Everything seemed the same visually. When they entered the door, it became clear. As clear as the glamorous Egyptian woman that darted up to Max and kissed him passionately, "Maximilian, I thought I'd never see you again!"

"Rachel, this is Tia."

"Hi," Rachel said, though her greeting was ignored as Tia knelt down in front of Max and prostrated herself once, lifted up, then bowed again.

"Huh..." Rachel looked for an explanation.

"I'm a bit of a deity to some of my creations," Max said sheepishly. This creation seemed laced with hubris, so much so that he was ashamed in front of this smart, stunning, and *real* woman.

"Stand, please, Tia. I see you've met up with Eco and Becca."

"Yes, they wanted me to do a few things for them, but I told them that I only answered to my master," Tia said with the pride of someone who knew that they had fulfilled their obligations.

Becca looked dourly at Max and clicked her tongue slightly, "Thanks for sending us here with such a dutiful rule-follower. It's been really fun trying to figure this crap out. Would an explanation really have killed you, *master*?"

"Sorry, I couldn't tell you much, but I knew you'd be safe here."

Tia didn't seem to be following Becca's passive aggressive meaning, or tracking the apology it prompted for Max, because she continued, "They asked me for a doorway. I told them that I only make doors for you, Max."

Max shrugged his shoulders towards Becca and Eco, "That's great, Tia. But, how did you become the key holder? You were my first creation here; I didn't think dad knew about you."

"Dan knew about everything," Tia proudly confessed. "He changed my programming to be the key holder, should you ever need one. I had strict instructions to never let you know unless you needed one."

"We need a door now Tia. Can you make one for us now?"

Eco, Becca, and Rachel all expected some sort of computer based activity. They even envisioned Tia summoning up some door with a wave of her hand. But, they didn't expect what came next. Tia looked down, clasped both hands together, and hummed for low tone for around three seconds. Then, she looked up and said loudly, *"When everything is natural, no one notices. When something is unnatural, everyone notices. Nature is the only place where nothing can be natural or unnatural because everything must coexist. There is power in paradox and it is the way to find what is natural and what is unnatural."*

"Wait," Becca said, "that's the riddle again."

"How is that supposed to help us now?" Eco turned towards Max. He looked as mystified as she did.

"I don't know. She can make doors, but I don't know how it works."

Tia spoke up cryptically, "All riddles have an answer."

"Where everything must coexist," Max said to himself. "I don't get it. Do we have to get it for the key?"

239

"Yes, you need to create the unnatural in nature," Tia said to the others, as if that would help them figure it out.

"That doesn't make sense. What's unnatural in nature?" Eco said with what was now overt anger dripping from each word. "And by the way, shouldn't we go get the others."

Max looked at his watch and thought for a second, "That was my intention, but I didn't know this would take so long. They are probably dead by now."

Just then, as if to offer a living refutation of his words, a light flashed that brought Zone and Dennis into the room.

"Zone! Dennis! Thank goodness you are okay," Eco said. "Where are the others?"

Zone feigned surprise and confusion pretty accurately, and responded to her question with one of his own, "Where are we?"

Max replied dryly, "That doesn't matter too much right now. Answer the question: where are the others?"

Dennis spoke up, "They all, I'm so sorry to say it…died on the Titanic."

It looked like Eco had been kicked in the gut. Rachel almost nodded, as if her fears had been confirmed. Becca, who'd felt very little loyalty to any of those people, neither spoke nor confirmed that she'd heard the news.

"It was all so fast," Zone continued. "They couldn't grab on, the ship was dissolving. We'd tried to…"

Tia did not clear her throat to interrupt Zone. She just started speaking, "No! That is not accurate. They killed them all with guns."

"Who the hell are you?" Zone asked angrily. "And why would you say such a thing?" he added, trying to act hurt by the harmful accusation.

"Liar!" Dennis piled on trying to convince them.

Tia did not seem to get upset by this disagreement or disdain. She just continued.

"I don't lie. I can't." She turned to Max, "They killed the others."

"It's true," Max said to the room. "Tia cannot lie. She can only speak the truth."

"But, why would you have killed them?" Eco said, her voice quavering.

"Well, it depends on what you mean by them," Zone replied as he and Dennis both pulled guns out from behind their backs. As they did so, Tia simultaneously jumped in front of Max to shield him from any possible harm.

This machine is really smart. Max thought to himself. *I never would have thought to tell it to do that. But, I appreciate the help!*

"With Dale, Brad, and Ron," Zone continued, "I killed them because they deserved it. They are responsible for my life as it stands, which is pretty much worthless and miserable. I figured that if I couldn't fix my life, I could fix those who screwed it up."

"I don't even know what you mean," Eco sobbed, "but what about Quest?"

"Quest just had a bit of bad luck. Wrong place. Really wrong time. Same with Baljeet."

"What have we done to you?" Becca challenged. "I was brought into this against my will."

"I agree, and I wasn't going to kill you," Zone commented. "But now you know too much, so you'll have to die as well. You can't really expect me to go back with you to reality and go to jail."

Both Eco and Becca asked at the same time, "Reality?"

Max ignored that question. Instead, he asked Dennis and Zone calmly, "Put the guns down, please. Let's talk about this. I'm sure we can figure out a solution in which everyone lives."

"No way. There will be no deal. No convincing, Max," Dennis said coolly. "Go ahead and start saying your goodbyes."

"Well, if that is your stance, let me explain something to Tia."

"Okay," Zone agreed, thinking that Max was going to say goodbye to this woman that they both agreed was indeed lovely.

"Tia. They want to kill me," Max whispered in her ear.

"Kill you?"

"Yes. Do you know what that means?"

Tia looked lovingly at Max, "Of course I do, Maximilian."

Becca hardly saw it. And, by it she didn't know how to explain what had happened after the fact. Eco, minutes later, was worthless in their attempt to unpack the events. She'd turned away and looked towards the windows at the precise moment it occurred. Only Rachel saw everything perfectly. She was standing just far enough from everyone to see things perfectly. She blinked first, and as her eyes opened she saw Tia say something to Max with a smile. Then, the beautiful Egyptian woman's facial expression changed subtly, ever so subtly, to one of dark purpose.

At the exact moment that her lips shifted downward, and her eyes changed from glow to glare, she flashed with movement. She moved the ten feet or so towards Zone with her hands outstretched. Into her right hand flashed metal, and suddenly she was holding a slender blade. *Did she summon that into existence?* Rachel wondered to herself as she watched that gleaming piece of steel sweep effortlessly across Zone's throat. Before the blood had even begun to spurt out of his neck, Tia had moved towards Dennis. No glint of light this time, just a drop of blood that flew from the sword's tip as it swept through the air from one victim to the next. Before either had processed what was happening, their necks were slashed. They gurgled, tried to clutch at their throats, but were on the ground in seconds. The flinching continued longer than their noises. No one in the room felt any sympathy as both Zone and Dennis Fast breathed their last breaths.

"Thank you, Tia." Max turned towards his assassin.

"You are welcome, my love. I'd do anything for you. I'd sacrifice myself for you if the occasion called for it." Tia responded as she retrieved a small towel out of the kitchen with which she wiped off the bloody blade.

"That will not be needed Tia. But…we do still need a way out."

Chapter 32

Max looked at the other women, a couple of which had just witnessed their first real life executions in person. Well, not real life per se, but the effects back in the real world had been real enough. Each of those women, save Rachel, seemed shaken greatly.

"I told you the key, Maximilian. That is all I am allowed to do."

"You created this place, and you didn't give yourself a way out you could understand?" Rachel asked Max testily.

"Hey! Cool it. Criticism isn't really the best creative fuel for me."

"Should I intervene, Max?" Tia asked as she glared threateningly at Rachel. For her part, Rachel wanted nothing of this lightning fast assassin.

"No need, Tia, no need. But, can you say the whole riddle one more time. I think I know it by heart but want to hear you say it once more."

"Of course," Tia nodded. *"When everything is natural, no one notices. When something is unnatural, everyone notices. Nature is the only place where nothing can be natural or unnatural because everything must coexist. There is power in paradox and it is the way to find what is natural and what is unnatural."*

"Um..." Becca started thinking out loud, "what if it means that something that is not natural in nature needs to be done?

Instead of changing our location, change the weather here, or something inappropriate."

"It's worth a shot," Max nodded and motioned for everyone to follow him outside. They walked outside to notice a beautiful sunset beginning over the lake. The reds of the sky echoed the reds of the trees, creating a visual impression that the air itself was bleeding.

"This place sure is pretty," Eco said.

"Pretty? It's perfect," replied Max. "What wouldn't be natural here?"

Eco spoke first, "How about buildings? Buildings would totally ruin this place."

Max turned to his computer and punched a few buttons, made a few swiping gestures. Suddenly, out in the distance to the right of the lake, up popped a couple of genuine skyscrapers. Eco and Becca, for their part, had given up on questioning everything that was going on. By this point, with so many deaths and unexplained events, were just rolling with it, hoping to maybe get an explanation if and when they got out alive.

"Certainly doesn't look natural here," Max said dourly.

They all stood and waited for something to appear. Nothing. Just the chirping of birds.

"You know Max, it may not look natural to you, especially with how familiar you are with this place. But, that kind of thing happens in the world. Places are developed all the time, despite the protestations of the friendly neighborhood environmentalists," joked Rachel. She offered her own suggestion, "How about something to do with the wildlife. This is a temperate region. You probably see a bunch of beavers, deer, squirrels, am I right?"

Tia nodded, "And a bear every now and then!"

"I bet you get ten snows a year at least, right, Tia? So, how about some rain forest animals? They'd have no place here."

Max grinned at Rachel's clever answer. He prodded his computer for a few minutes, and they all looked up to see, and hear, Howler Monkeys cutting up in the nearby spruce trees. In the lake below them, out crawled smaller versions of alligators to find what was left of the sun. The water would have been far too cold for them and they moved sluggishly.

"Caiman!" Eco said. "They are like tiny alligators. I saw them once in Costa Rica."

At the bare dogwood tree that stood close by, a Toucan swept up and perched. It cawed loudly.

"You asked for some animals I believe?" Max took great pride in his achievement. "Next I'll summon some *Fruit Loops* to match the bird."

"It's neat, Max," Rachel assured him, though she wondered how often in the future she should encourage that ego.

"But we are still here…" Becca reminded him.

"Too true, Becca. Must not have been 'unnatural' enough. All of these animals have counterparts here of some sort, save the monkeys. Any other ideas?"

"Change the weather, Maximilian." Tia spoke quietly from the doorway where she still stood observing.

Max thought for a second. He started to turn towards his computer twice, then stopped short. Finally, he turned to the others.

"What is the most unnatural weather system for a place like this?" he asked the group.

"Hurricanes? We are in the mountains after all."

"Earthquakes!"

Max registered those two suggestions and turned again to his computer. He punched a few buttons and looked up.

"Watch this!" he said.

From the ground in the distance, up swept what looked to be a lighter version of the forest. Whereas the spruce and bushes were all deep greens, this was more of a light khaki color. And, each of the people noticed quickly, it was headed towards them!

"What have you done Max?"

"Sandstorm!" he said with no small bit of giddy in his voice.

Both Becca and Rachel turned away from the approaching storm as individual grains started to pepper them. Eco, in glasses, stood a bit longer, watching the whipping winds build. The sounds grew deafening as the sand started to hit the house behind them, and trees creaked and cracked in each direction. Max stood firmly, his eyes squinting, watching to see if this crazy idea would work. From beyond the lake, he saw a white light. It flashed toward them with the sand.

Max shouted, "What is that?"

"There is your key!" Tia yelled from behind him.

As her words echoed in his ears, Max and the others flashed from this scenic—if oddly weathered—locale back into a bustling office building.

"What the hell!" Becca heard a man's voice replace the deafening storm.

She looked up to see the room in which she'd landed. Around her were the three guards that had been in the room when she departed.

"Time Vacation?" she asked the guy standing nearest her.

"This is the Time Vacation building," he replied, "of course. You were just here Ms. Baxter."

"Home!" she breathed a sigh of relief.

"Where are the others?" the commander of the men asked.

Becca patted herself to make sure everything had arrived safely. She'd never felt so excited to be in a room with three men she loathed.

"Damn it, woman. Answer me. Where are the others? Where is Dale Brooks?"

"Open his pod and find out," Becca said curtly. He walked up to a pod and pressed the large green button to the left of the doorway. It slid open smoothly and quietly. As it opened, out fell the Dale in question. He hit the floor hard, his head thudding loudly.

"Shit! Mr. Brooks!" said the commander.

He then knelt down to check Dale's pulse. Finding no sign of life, he turned to the other pods. With each he opened, out slumped another dead person. Brad Hammer. Baljeet. Dennis Fast.

"What the hell happened to these guys?"

Becca shrugged her shoulders, "You all kidnapped me. You have fun explaining it to your bosses or the authorities. I'm leaving."

Shocked and slightly afraid of the fact that she alone had survived something very strange and mysterious, none of the guards stopped Becca Baxter as she stormed past them and headed towards the elevator.

The place in which Max and Rachel arrived was entirely different from the one in which Becca set down. But, it looked exactly the same as the place from which they'd just come.

"Your cottage!" Rachel exclaimed happily.

"The one in our world?" Eco asked, still a great deal of confusion in her voice.

"Where's Becca?" Rachel asked.

"At the main office. Where her pod was," Max replied.

"She's safe?"

"I'm sure of it. I would imagine the guards there will be so shocked to find the corpses that they'll let her walk. They might think she is some sort of magical witch or something!" Max laughed.

"Now what?" Rachel asked.

"Now," Max paused to summon up every ounce of resolve, "We destroy everything."

"Destroy it?" Eco asked.

"I hate the idea too. But this is far too dangerous to keep around anymore. I think most of my creations may have been flawed with all of the jumps anyways. I'd feel reluctant to go back for fear of getting caught in some sort of loop or glitch. The entire thing may be too damaged to repair anyway."

"I agree, Max." Rachel urged him on, "Destroy it."

"The system is tied into the main frame at Time Vacation. I can wipe the computers clean from here."

"All your women?"

Max looked at Rachel and smiled, "I only need one."

Rachel blushed, but Eco looked back and forth at both of them dumbly.

"What in the world are y'all talking about? Please explain just what the hell happened in there."

"Eco, there are a few things you should know about time travel..." Max laughed.

Chapter 33

It was a bright and sunny afternoon and the fishing was good. Max had only been out for a couple hours and already he had plenty for the evening's dinner. The best fishing was still to come, too, as the sun climbed further into the sky and closer to sunset. As he looked towards the shore, though, Max suddenly didn't feel like fishing any more that day. A vision of his future pulled him back to the docks.

As he rowed back, Rachel leaned up from the towel upon which she was laying. She rested her head upon her hands and arched her back to look towards Max.

"Fishing over for the day?"

"I've got a date!" He replied.

"Date?" she answered playfully.

"Yup, with a nice glass of Scotch."

"So funny Max. Anything else you couldn't stay away from?"

"Ah…of course, I also have a date with one lovely lady."

"Aww," Rachel cooed sarcastically.

Max climbed out of the boat and walked over to Rachel. She rolled over to her back to look up towards him and he knelt down to kiss her on the cheek.

"Rachel, isn't real life here as good as anything that could have happened in there?"

"This is impossible to beat!" she nodded. "I'm just surprised that you gave it all up for me, honey."

"For something real? It was worth it. *Really* worth it!" Max said as he leaned over to kiss her this time on the lips.

"And, there's something else that is coming soon. It'll be real enough for both of us!" Rachel giggled as she pulled Max to her stomach, which was growing larger daily.

"We may need a slightly bigger place," Max said.

"I can't wait."

About the Author

Leif J. Erickson was born and raised on a grain farm outside Wheaton, MN, just a stone's throw from White Rock, SD, which served as the inspiration for the Ghost Town series. From a very early age, Leif knew that he was going to be a farmer, just like his father and grandfather. As he grew up, Leif learned everything he could about farming, always riding in equipment with his dad and helping out wherever he could.

After Leif graduated high school he attended North Dakota State University in Fargo, North Dakota, where he achieved a BS in Agricultural Economics along with a minor in History. During his time in college, Leif networked with many other farmers from across North Dakota, South Dakota, and Minnesota, while advancing his knowledge in all aspects of agricultural. With a diploma in hand, Leif returned to the family farm and started his career as a farmer.

The first season was very successful and stood as a testament to the hard work and education that Leif had received. All signs pointed to a lifetime career as a farmer until a family tragedy struck and the family farm was dispersed. For the first time in his life, Leif didn't know what he wanted to pursue for a career.

Leif returned to Fargo, ND where he began his career as a stock and futures trader. It was during this time that he began to become serious about writing. With one computer watching the markets, Leif would be on the other, writing. Leif quickly realized though that Fargo wasn't the city or location that he wanted to make a home in. Less than one year since he moved there, Leif moved to Plymouth MN, in the Twins Cities area.

Continuing with the trading and writing, Leif began to learn everything that he could about writing, about storytelling, and about the hero's journey. Leif spent his spare time reading novels or books about writing. It was during his time in the Cities that Leif wrote many, many different stories, getting the outlines and first drafts finished. In the three years that Leif was in the Cities, he wrote the first draft for over fifty different stories.

Leif received information about a career opportunity that was back in his hometown of Wheaton so he returned to go to work for the local grain elevator. The work was hard and the days were long without much time for writing. Leif missed being able to write every day. He had so many more stories that he wanted to write. Being aggressive and a hard worker, Leif quickly moved up the ladder in the company and within six months he was in a management position.

Although Leif had met and dated many women when he was in the Twin Cities, it was in Wheaton where he met the new Science Teacher at his old High School and within fifteen months of meeting the pair were married at Good Shepherd Lutheran Church in Wheaton. Many have described the pair as absolutely made for each other, and they spend much of their time hiking in State Parks or canoeing the local lakes and rivers.

Being back in Wheaton, Leif used his free time to polish up and finish some of his stories. He got two stories to the point where he was satisfied to bring them to the marketplace and share them with others. Although he still works for the elevator, Leif looks forward to the day when he can write fulltime, offering more novels and screenplays to entertain and delight others.

During his life, Leif was always quick to be able to tell a story. He had an uncanny ability to quickly make up a story on the spot (sometimes to the dismay of parents and teachers) and to pull people into the story with wild characters, amazing locations, and fantastical storylines. Although Leif focuses on science fiction, he's written stories in many different genera's including mystery, horror, teen comedy, western, and even a little romance.

Throughout Leif's writings you can see traces of his farm life and his love of nature. Being an ecologist and former farmer, much of Leif's writings feature forests, lakes, and nature in general. Leif has always been interested in science and what's possible for the human race, pushing the envelope of technologies, and finding how far humans can go. Much of Leif's science fiction writing explores these themes and ideas.

When he's not writing, Leif and his wife Brittany can be found working on their goal of hiking in every State Park in Minnesota or on the lakes and rivers in a canoe. The pair have some big canoe adventures planned, and have already canoed, from end to end, big lakes such as Lake Traverse and Big Stone Lake. Every once in a while, Leif will pull out his old Disc Jockey system and play a dance as the 'Leif of the Party DJ Service.'

Leif has been influenced by many different writers and stories. His all-time favorite story is 'Sleepy Hollow' by Washington Irving, a story that Leif reads every Halloween. Other influences on his work are the 'Dune' series by Frank Herbert, 'The Lord of the Rings' by J.R.R. Tolkien, and anything related to the Arthurian Legend. Leif also enjoys many other authors such as Charles Dickens, Michael Crichton, John Steinbeck, Isaac Asimov, Neil Gaiman, and F. Scott Fitzgerald just to name a few.

Thank you for checking out a book by Leif Erickson. Please visit his website at www.leifericksonwriting.com and purchase the other books that Leif has written. They will take you on a journey that you will never forget…